LEAVING TO STAY

A Rock Star Bad Boy Babies Romance

NICOLE CASEY

Copyright © 2018 by Nicole Casey. All Rights Reserved.

Without limiting the rights under copyright reserved above, no part of this publication may be reproduced, stored, or introduced into a retrieval system, or transmitted in any form, or by any means (electronically, mechanical, photocopying, recording or otherwise) without the proper written permission of the copyright owner, except in the case of brief quotations embodied in critical articles and reviews.

This book is a work of fiction. People, places, events and situations are the product of the author's imagination. Any resemblance to actual persons, living or dead, or historical events, is purely coincidental.

CONTENTS

Prologue	1
1. Jude	13
2. Geneva	27
3. Jude	45
4. Geneva	59
5. Jude	73
6. Geneva	87
7. Jude	99
8. Jude	111
9. Geneva	123
10. Geneva	131
11. Geneva	141
12. Jude	153
13. Jude	167
14. Geneva	181
15. Jude	195
Epilogue	205
Letter to the readers	215
Sneak Peek: Accidental Soulmates	219
Also By Nicole Casey	293
About the Author	295

PROLOGUE

Geneva

I stared at the newspaper for a long time, the ink staining my fingers as I flipped through it. Yet I kept going back to the article, my heart sick with betrayal.

It was obscene reading it in print like that, as if it made it all that much more real than seeing it on TMZ's website.

He did it. He really went ahead with it without so much as a second thought.

I don't know why I was surprised or disappointed. I knew what he was capable of – I had from the very start. I had no one to blame but myself for the outcome. How much warning did

I need? How much foresight was enough for someone like me? Never enough apparently.

Daddy would give you that knowing look right now if he was here, I thought, shuddering slightly at the image of his intense brown eyes boring into me. *But he'd tell me to suck it up and move on with my life and that's what I'll do. I've wasted enough time being angry at him. I can't fault a snake for being a snake after all.*

Of course, it was easy for Daddy to say things like that. Life had always rolled off his shoulders without any regard for anyone else.

My cell phone dinged again and I sighed heavily, glancing at the screen.

It was Elsa for the third time but I didn't want to speak with her. I didn't want to speak with anyone. I couldn't deal with the pitying tones and the pseudo support.

In my mind's ear, I could already hear their words verbatim.

"You should go down there and…"

"He doesn't deserve this and you do…"

"If I were you, I'd…"

Yeah, I knew. I knew what they were going to say and what they'd do if they were in my position but they weren't. They were on the outside, looking sadly in and I was the same confused girl I'd sworn I'd never be again.

This was my burden to bear and I refused to bear it anymore.

Sighing, I rose from the couch and padded across the trailer toward the kitchenette to grab another beer from the fridge.

It would be my fourth but no one would have known. If I was going to drown my bitterness that night, I was going to need something much stronger than Bud.

I wasn't even sure when my tolerance had escalated to the point it had. Once upon a time, two beers would have been my limit for the night. Suddenly, I was a full-fledged lush.

As I popped the cap off the beer and pressed it to my lips, someone pounded on the flimsy door and I stifled a groan.

Shit!

Of course, the next course of action would be just showing up on my doorstep. I should have hidden myself better but it was too late to consider that now; the blinds were open and the lights were on.

Music was playing, albeit softly, from my laptop's speakers but the walls were stupidly thin in the trailer, something else I'd learned the hard way a long time ago.

"Gen, we know you're in there!" Marybeth called. "I've got Elsa and Carrie with me."

Double shit. They're all here.

There was no way to avoid them; if I didn't let them in, they'd just break in. It wasn't hard and my neighbors certainly weren't going to call the cops. They'd probably all pull up lawn chairs and watch the action. God knows, nothing else of interest happened in Elizabeth.

"Gen – "

I shoved open the door, catching them off balance but they didn't tumble from the rickety steps.

"What are you doing here?" I asked rhetorically. Of course, it was a dumb question but it was the first one that sprung from my lips. Maybe I'd had too much to drink after all because I was suddenly feeling a little light headed.

I really could have done without the company of my angry friends, well-meaning as they were.

The problem was, I didn't even know if I was as enraged as they were. I may have reached the pinnacle of apathy by that point. Either that or the alcohol was doing its job. In any case, I would have rather they not have been there but it didn't matter; there was nothing I could do about them being there now.

"What did you think was going to happen if you didn't answer your phone?" Carrie retorted, pushing her way past me, wrinkling her nose as she looked inside my unkempt residence. "Christ, Geneva, how long has it been since you opened a window in here? Is something dead?"

Just my soul, I thought brightly.

"All the windows are opened!" I protested but I wasn't sure if that was true. I'd been fermenting in the trailer for six weeks at least, barely making it out for groceries. Thankfully, I'd found a beer delivery service, willing to come out my way.

"Good lord!" Elsa muttered, stepping over a pile

of discarded clothes, including a pile of dirty underwear. "Baby, you have got to go take a shower. I'll clean up in here."

"Girls, I know you mean well – "

"We ain't goin' anywhere, Gen," Marybeth told me. "You better get used to it and go have a shower."

I opened my mouth to argue again but I changed my mind, knowing that the three against one was not going to fare well for me.

"Just go have a shower," Elsa said gently, shooing me toward the closet-sized bathroom off the bedroom. "We'll be here when you come out."

That was motivation enough to escape into the shower. It would buy me time away from their well-meaning but overbearing presence.

I stripped off my clothes and stepped through the accordion door, realizing how rank I was. God, how long had it been since I'd bathed?

I was aghast at myself, a deep humiliation flushing through my neck and staining my cheeks crimson. I couldn't believe I'd let them see me like this, especially Carrie and Marybeth who barely knew me.

Ire overtook my embarrassment, the thought of how much time I'd wasted moping about the past month and a half consuming me like a wave of nausea.

Damn it! He's off living the dream and I'm sulking around like a teenager who lost her first boyfriend to college. This ends today. He doesn't deserve my woe. He doesn't even deserve my thoughts.

As the shower ran, steaming up the closed space, the bile bubbling in my throat refused to go down and I knew then that I was going to vomit.

It's too hot in here, I thought, dropping to my knees, my head over the toilet. I retched, spitting up what little I'd eaten that day but my stomach wouldn't stop churning.

Great. And now I'm going to get sick on top of everything else.

"Baby? You okay in there?" Marybeth called. "You're gettin' sick?"

"I'm fine!" I yelled back.

"You sure?"

"Yeah."

Slowly, nausea subsided and I stepped under the cooling water, scrubbing the dirt and sweat from my lithe body with ferociousness.

I had waited too long to jump in and I had a limited supply of hot water depleted in minutes but I had to admit that when I got out, I was feeling a lot more human than I had before getting in.

Snatching a towel off a plastic hook, I wrapped myself in the frayed material, chestnut waves dripping down my back as I let myself out of the bathroom. Before I could hang a right into my cramped bedroom, I caught a glimpse my posse of friends staring at me in a horizontal line across the living room, their heads cocked sideways.

They were studying me with embarrassing closeness.

"What?" I asked, my brow knitting. "Did you find a rat or something? Did something actually die in here? Because I swear, I didn't know about it."

I was joking but they didn't smile, their faces an identical mask of concern.

"Get dressed," Elsa said. "And then we'll talk."

"No, you're making me nervous," I insisted. "What?"

"Baby, we don't wantcha to take this the wrong way but – "

"When was the last time your Aunt Flo visited?" Carrie interjected bluntly, cutting off Marybeth midsentence.

My chocolate eyes widened.

"What?" I asked, a small smile curving over my lips. "What are you asking me?"

"Baby, is there any chance you're knocked up?"

"What?" I howled with laughter and turned away from them to retreat into my bedroom for an outfit.

"Um, Jude has been gone for months," I reminded them. "And as hard as this is to believe, men aren't really lining up at my door."

But as the words left my lips, I paused, staring at my naked reflection in the full-length mirror.

My body had changed in small, subtle ways. My stomach wasn't as flat. God! Were my hips wider?

I had noticed tenderness in my breasts but that was common before my time of month...

When had that last been?

I gasped and whirled around, my pupils dilating as my girls gathered in the doorway, worry etched in their expressions.

"Oh, Gen," Elsa sighed, hurrying toward me, embracing me. "It's all right, honey. We'll figure this out."

But I shook my head in denial.

God, no! I screamed silently. *This ain't happening. He doesn't get to steal my dream and abandon me with a baby. I am not that girl! I will never be that girl!*

Another round of sickness seized me and I pushed out of Elsa's grasp and floundered toward the toilet.

When I had finished retching, sitting back against the still damp walls, I looked up dumbly at my friends, trying to think of something to say.

"Gen..." Elsa tried again, her mothering instinct kicking in as she crouched down but I shook my head, my jaw twitching.

If I didn't want to hear their platitudes before, I was violently opposed to hearing them in this instance.

"Someone needs to get to CVS," I said, mustering every ounce of calm I could into my voice. "And get me a kit."

They seemed to snap into action at once, each one tripping over the other toward the door as if they could sense the fury emanating from my bones.

And I envied them at that moment because they could leave.

I didn't need a stick to tell me what I had been avoiding for weeks.

I was going to have a baby, and I was going to be just like so many other girls we'd known.

Gone were my aspirations of being a singer and songwriter.

I was destined to be a single mom, living in a trailer park with a baby daddy who never knows his kid.

1
JUDE

My brow furrowed as I strummed again, adjusting my fingers to the frets but it still didn't sound right.

"G or A?" I asked Brutus but the Rottweiler didn't even bother to raise his massive head to acknowledge me.

I didn't really blame him. It was hotter than hell out that morning and it wasn't even close to noon yet.

I couldn't imagine what it was like to have an all-black body covered in fur under the Louisiana heat so I didn't take it personally when he didn't seem to have any opinion on my new song.

I wasn't sure I even had an opinion about it either.

"Baby, can we go now?" Kristy moaned. "I'm meltin' out here!"

"One sec," I told her without raising my head. I had almost forgotten she was there, the tune absorbing my concentration although, in hindsight, I'm not sure how I could have overlooked her presence.

Her shrill voice had busted my concentration, at least for the time being and while I tried to regain the momentum of what I was working on, it had escaped like a heated vapor off the bayou.

"Baby," she whined again and I glanced up at her, my green eyes flashing with annoyance.

"All right!" I snapped, gently casting the instrument onto the scarred wooden bench on the porch. "Let's go!"

Immediately, her demeanor changed as she sensed my irritation and she gave me a beguiling look, her blue eyes wide and innocent.

"Honey, you can keep workin' if you're in a groove," she said, doing a complete about-face but the moment had passed and I rose to my full height, casting a shadow on her wiry form.

Kristy had been a fixture in my life since childhood, the girl next-door in a sense and most everyone in Oakdale wrongly assumed we were a couple.

It was more because Kristy drove that impression home, her claws firmly digging into my broad shoulders like the talons of an eagle despite the fact that I had made it very clear for years that we would never be together like that.

I guess it didn't help that I let her hang around and continued to sleep with her but Oakdale was a small town and the pickings weren't great. She was the closest thing to a single "town beauty" as Oakdale could come by so I wasn't about to toss her to the curb just yet.

One day, I'll move to New York and I won't have to worry about Kristy McClellan's chili cheese fry cravings.

"Just meet me in the truck," I sighed, tossing her the keys out of my pocket. "I'll be out in a minute."

She caught the set with one hand and offered me a broad grin, spinning to sashay away in what she likely thought was a provocative sway in her frayed jean shorts and halter top but watching her only fueled my aggravation.

Maybe it was the heat but she seemed to be getting on my nerves more than usual the past week or so.

It was probably time to schedule another "break up" which, truly, was more of a "time out." I required breathing room from Kristy every once in a while and the summer was a good a time as any to take it. Sometimes tourists moseyed in through Oakdale while traveling through the state and there was nothing quite like a summer fling.

I slipped back into the cottage-style house which I shared with Jimmy Chase and wandered toward the bathroom. To my chagrin, my roommate was already in there.

What else is new?

"Jim, you gonna be long?" I called, checking my exasperation.

"Yep."

I smothered a groan.

"How long?"

"No idea."

He was a third cousin of mine or twice removed or some craziness that only a grandmother with too many cats and too much free time could decipher. I knew that I was supposed to appreciate him as a member of my family but his one-word answers and bathroom hogging was getting to be a bit much after two years of living together.

Yeah, I was cranky.

"Heading to Buster's," I offered, trying to check my temper. "Want me to bring you anything?"

"Nope."

I did grunt that time, spinning toward my bedroom to slide some deodorant under my arms and put on a shirt.

My bladder would have to hold until we got into town.

I dug out an old Nirvana t-shirt and slipped it over my smooth, bronze chest, covering the litany of tattoos instantly as my arms found the sleeves.

As my head poked through the neck hole, I

caught sight of myself in the mirror over the dresser and I paused to squint at my face.

My bright emerald eyes seemed to depict my internal state of mind, flashing with mild indignation beneath a flood of thick, black eyelashes.

I hadn't shaved in a couple days, a dirty-blonde scruff covering my face, the strands of my matching head of shoulder length hair catching in the stubble as I peered closer.

Was I getting crow's feet?

It seemed impossible. I was only twenty-eight and in great shape. I worked out every day in some form whether swimming in the Calcasieu River or actually hitting the gym to push my own mass in weights.

I ate all right, stuck to hard liquor to avoid the beer gut and even that I did in moderation...for a country boy anyway.

My mouth became a grimace of disgust and I exhaled in a long whoosh as I realized that it was just a trick of the lighting; there were no wrinkles.

Getting older was a touchy subject for me, probably because I had always thought I would be in a completely different place by my age.

My biggest fear was being a washed-up musician, busking on subway platforms at forty but it seemed that was where I was headed.

Or worse, that I would be trapped in Oakdale for the rest of my life, raising half a dozen kids with Kristy McClellan.

The sound of the truck's horn shattered my self-pitying moment and I grabbed my wallet from the dressed to meet her.

I'm gonna buy her some chili cheese fries and then I'm gonna dump her. Again.

∽

BUSTER'S WAS ODDLY BUSY FOR A WEEKDAY but I realized it was lunchtime. I hoped that we didn't run into anyone we knew but the chances of that were slim to none. It *was* Oakdale after all. It was not known for a place to be incognito.

As we collected our orders and sat at a picnic table near the stagnant pond, I gazed over Kristy's shoulder at the swans floating through the glassy water as if they were the most interesting thing in the world.

Anything to avoid listening to Kristy's incessant babbling about her classes at Louisiana Tech. She was so proud of her community college education, it embarrassed me.

That's the best anyone in this town can hope for. A community college degree and suckering some unsuspecting idiot into marriage.

"Baby, you should think about taking some courses too," she offered, directly on schedule. It was her goal to "better" me. She couldn't fathom that I would want to work a menial job tending the lawns at Oakdale Cemetery while working on my music.

"It's a great hobby, baby, but what are you gonna do with your life?" she would inevitably ask and each time she did, my hands would close into a fist and I'd dig my nails into my palms until they bled.

Oh, God. Not Again. How could I expect her to understand? She didn't have an artistic bone in her body. No one in that God forsaken town did.

The best we could find for live entertainment

was karaoke night at Sylvester Cat's although I had been granted gigs in some of the smaller bars on occasion.

The problem was, no one cared for listening to soulful rock tunes, especially not when the musician was a kid they'd known since he was stealing lollipops from the general store.

Right. It's impossible to be taken seriously in this one-horse town. I need to get the fuck outta here before those crow's feet actually become more than figments of my imagination.

"Baby!"

I looked at her reluctantly, knowing I hadn't heard a word she said.

"What?"

She sat back, her straw blonde hair falling over her bony shoulders as she folded her arms under her breasts.

"I don't understand you!" she complained. "Why do I even bother?"

Lack of options? Glutton for punishment? Stupidity? Creature of habit?

Of course, I didn't volunteer any of my theories.

"Why are you upset now?" I sighed. "If this is about going to school, I've already told you I'm not going back. I already have a degree in musical engineering and producing from Tulane in case you've forgotten."

Why did I feel the need to bring that up? It had to have been more for my own benefit than hers, a reminder that I had not wasted my life up to this point. I still had a degree which I did absolutely nothing with.

It was as if she had read my mind.

"And look whatcha doin' with your life!" she protested. "You're mowin' graves for the love of God!"

She was giving me the out I needed and I took it with glee. I needed to get it done. Right. Fucking. Now. This was going to be the easiest break up ever. She was going to be the asshole this time, and that always made things so much easier.

But before I could play my "hurt" card, she leaned forward to clasp my hands in hers, catching me off guard.

"I have a plan for us, babe, but you have to work with me."

"For us?" I echoed. "Kristy, you and I do not have a future. How many times have we had this conversation?"

She smirked at me and the expression on her face unnerved me slightly.

"Just hear me out, baby. I'll be done my practical nursin' degree at the end of next year," Kristy explained. "I should have no problem getting a job right away. My grades are really good. I start workin' and you can go back to school. I think you'll be great at IT stuff. You like electronics and stuff, right?"

I don't know how I managed not to roll my eyes but I was impressed with my composure.

"Then, after you graduate, we can get married and we can start a family right away!"

I choked, spitting out a piece of my burger onto the table before her and she eyed it with disgust as I tried to catch my breath.

"What the hell is that?" she snapped. "Ain'tcha sowed enough of your wild oats, Jude? I ain't never said anythin' when you fucked half the town. I understood that you needed to get it out of your system but enough is enough! When are you gonna settle down, be a man?"

A stab of anger flooded through me and not for the first time, I felt like throwing something at her head. Not to cause damage, of course, but just to knock some sense into her ditzy brain, see if there was actually anything working in there.

"You really don't know a damn thing about me, do you?" I growled, rising from the bench. I tossed my napkin on my half-eaten meal, my appetite gone. "I'm not going back to school, and I sure as hell am not marrying you!"

"You'll change your mind," she said confidently. "Maybe we'll try for a baby first."

I gaped at her, the desire to laugh at the ludicrousness of her words overwhelming.

"Fuck. Kristy, I'm going now," I told her firmly. "And you need to stay away from me now. I'm sorry if you have truly believed that we're going to be together but you've never been more wrong about anything in your life."

I didn't give her a chance to respond, spinning to leave her at the table alone but I heard her last words to me as I stalked away, my mind spinning dubiously.

"You'll be back," she called. "You always come back."

Not this time, I thought grimly. *This time she's finally hit my crazy threshold. Babies! Has she lost her damned mind? I'll never have kids with her or anyone else. There is not a woman alive who could ever change my mind.*

2
GENEVA

I wiped the sweat from my brow and plopped heavily against the side of the U-Haul, shaking my dark waves so that they fluttered over my eyes.

"Holy hell," I gasped, looking in disbelief at my belongings. "When did I become a materialist?"

Elsa laughed her tinkling chuckle.

"Honey, if you think you've got a lot of stuff, you've never been to my place," she replied, grabbing a box off the curb.

"Well, moving a two-bedroom condo into a sixteen by sixteen trailer makes me feel like I'm the princess of Monaco right now. What the hell was I thinking? I should have rented a storage unit."

"You were thinking that you needed to get out of Nashville before you got swallowed up by the industry," my best friend reminded me. "This is just the break you need, sweetie. So, what if you're downsizing a little? It's only temporary, remember?"

I remembered what I had told her and myself but I didn't know if that was the truth. Leaving Nashville was one of the hardest decisions I'd ever had to make and I was still reeling from the abruptness of my choice.

"Come on, Gen. We've only got a few more things to bring inside and then I'll bring you back to my place," Else urged. "You can stay with us tonight and deal with this mess tomorrow."

I looked at her gratefully and reached for one of the last cartons on the dirt, following her toward my new home.

It wasn't anything special, certainly not in comparison to the two-bedroom, two-bathroom suite I'd left behind but I certainly couldn't complain about the updated trailer on the outskirts of Elizabeth.

Honestly, I was surprised by brother had maintained it as well as he had, given the rocky relationship he'd had with my dad before our old man had passed.

Marc had been thrilled when I told him I was moving back to Louisiana and he almost screamed with joy when I told him I was going to take the trailer for a little while.

"Hallelujah!" he cried. "I'm so damned sick of going up there to make sure the rednecks haven't torched it."

"Not a ringing endorsement from a safety perspective, Marc," I said dryly. "Why don't you move it closer to Lafayette?"

"And have a constant reminder of that bastard in my backyard? No thank you. If you want, I can make the arrangements though. It really ain't that safe a place."

"I'll see how it goes," I replied. I didn't have the heart to tell him that Nashville wasn't exactly Hollywood, no matter how much they tried to portray it as such in the media. I could throw down with the worst of them if need be. A bunch of old hicks in a rundown trailer park were hardly at the top of my list of danger.

The truth was, I was happy to be away from

people. Nashville had sucked the life out of me entirely, crushing the optimistic spirit I'd gone with and turned me bitter.

Or at least I felt bitter inwardly. Elsa didn't seem to notice any change in me but the fact I had stepped up my wardrobe with knock-off Louboutin's and a fake Chanel purse.

She knew a little bit about why I had come back home, or at least home-ish, but she didn't know all the gory details. And I wasn't ready to spill them all either.

Luckily for me, Elsa was not one to pry and she was happy to have me home. And I had to admit, it felt good to be missed. I hadn't been the best at upkeeping our relationship but Elsa had opened her heart as she always had since we were kids, welcoming me home with her usual kind spirit.

I placed the last of my goods onto the little bit of space I could find in the kitchen and looked around, sighing aloud.

"It's not that bad!" Elsa insisted. "Jake and I are just down the road and it has everything you need!"

She didn't need to sell me on its merits. I already knew them.

"I am not complaining," I insisted. "But I'm disgusting and I need a shower. Let me see if I can dig up some fresh clothes and – "

"Never mind all that," Elsa interrupted. "You and I are still more or less the same size. I have everything you need, including a jacuzzi tub. You have to be exhausted after all that travel and Jake promised ribs you won't soon forget."

I smiled sheepishly at the blonde, my heart welling with affection for her as I studied her doll-like profile.

She really was the quintessential southern belle, born and raised in New Orleans like me but to blue blood parents who had ensured she attended the finest schools and had the best of everything.

Jake Henderson had not been their daughter's first or even tenth choice for Elsa but she had bravely risked disinheritance to marry the contractor and live her version of happily ever after in Oakdale.

Of course, I mused, *I wasn't exactly Mr.and Mrs.*

Sawhill's first choice for Elsa's best friend either, was I?

Not that I could blame Elsa's parents. The fact they didn't like me probably had less to do with the fact my family wasn't rich than it did that I was a rebel without a cause and constantly being rescued by their angelic daughter.

I think I still owed Elsa some bail money from one of my shoplifting endeavors from '07.

That was a long time ago, I told myself firmly. *I'm an independent woman now. I've seen the world learned what's out there. I don't need anyone to take care of me anymore. I can take care of myself.*

"Ready?" she asked, catching my gaze and I nodded.

"For southern homestyle ribs? You bet your sweet little ass I am!" I laughed.

I locked the trailer, casting one last look around the trailer park.

I was home. For now.

Why did that fill me with a familiar sense of dread?

∽

I hadn't been to Henderson's house in years, not since I'd first left for Nashville and I was stunned at what they had done to the property.

"Holy hell!" I choked as Elsa's SUV pulled through the quaint archway gate of their sprawling ranch-style home. "It's twice the size it was!"

"I keep forgetting you haven't been here in five years," she laughed. "Jake, God bless him, is convinced that we're going to be living here with our grandchildren one day and he just keeps adding to it."

I felt a strange pang in my chest when she said that and I cast her a sidelong look.

How do people still believe in love like that in this day and age? Elsa always did love those fairy tale themed parties. And I always dressed like the wicked stepmother in black, gothic.

But I could see that Elsa had just as much faith in their union as her husband and it warmed me, even though the cynic in me wondered a bunch of terrible things.

I had been convinced that their marriage would fall apart after the birth of their daughter. Kids always ruined marriages, after all. That's always the tipping point.

But Cath was two now and Elsa and Jake seemed to still be going strong.

Maybe after baby number two, I mused. I wondered if there was something psychologically wrong with me to think in such a way. There had to be.

I shushed the voices in my head and focused on the picturesque entranceway, barely noting that there were at least six vehicles in the circle drive until Elsa mentioned it.

"I can sneak you in the front since everyone is gonna be in the yard by the pool," she volunteered. "I'll get you all set up and you can make a grand entrance."

I blinked, suddenly understanding that it was not going to be a quiet dinner at home as I had expected.

There were going to be people there. Lots of them.

"Oh, Else, what did you do?" I groaned. If I'd known that it was a party, I would have opted out that night but I suspected that was why Elsa hadn't mentioned it in the first place.

"It's just a few friends," she promised. "People you're gonna meet anyway. Nothing fancy and no reason to be nervous."

"I'm not nervous," I grumbled. "I'm tired and I don't feel like being on my best behavior."

Elsa laughed, bringing the brand-new Ford Edge to a stop and turning to me.

"Baby, I've never seen you on your best behavior in my life. Don't pretend that a couple small town folks are gonna make you uncomfortable."

I forced a smile and nodded. She wasn't wrong; tact was not my strong suit but she was entirely missing the point.

She meant well and she didn't understand that I'd spent the last five years of my life smiling and nodding, bending over backward to accommodate others to the point of self-detriment. The last thing I wanted was to plaster a fake grin on my face and do it all over again, not even for a few hours.

I kept my reservations to myself.

"Come on," Elsa urged. "Before someone sees

us sitting out here. Those Louboutin's aren't going to distract from your dirt-streaked face for long."

"You know they're fake, right?"

"Of course I do, sugar. Same as that purse."

She was teasing me but I knew she was right; I desperately needed a shower. I felt bad that she'd been stuck sitting so close to me in the fifteen-minute drive from Elizabeth.

We snuck in the foyer quietly and I barely had time to take in the workmanship of the double banisters leading up to a mezzanine balcony level through marble stairs. Elsa whisked me away through one of the twin corridors leading to the east side of the house.

"Is Cath here?" I asked when she threw open the double doors to a beautiful, white carpeted suite.

"She's probably in bed but you'll meet her tomorrow," Elsa promised as I gawked at the bedroom. "Don't you worry. There will be plenty of time to get to see her now that you're home."

A large canopy, embraced in filmy curtains stole

the center of the room on a pedestal, facing a stone fireplace.

Of course, it was far too hot a day to light it but I could only imagine what a glow it cast when night fell and the lights were out.

"The bathroom is through that door," Elsa pointed. "I'll run upstairs and find you a bikini and something to wear while you bathe. Use the jets."

I grinned at her and shook my head.

"If I jump into a bath with jacuzzi jets right now, there are no guarantees I'm coming out," I warned her.

She eyed me speculatively for a silent moment and I instantly was filled with shame.

"I'm just kidding!" I laughed. "I'll be there with bells on!"

I hurried toward the bathroom, again wondering what was wrong with me.

She's been amazing to you and you're acting like a spoiled brat. Get it together and be grateful you have her when everyone else has crawled back into the woodwork.

I shut off all my misgivings and tried to appreciate the opulence of the six-piece bathroom.

A bidet? Really?

I had to grin at the touch, knowing it was probably never used.

I will bet my life's savings that Jake doesn't even know how to use that thing, I chuckled silently.

There was no way I was going to soak in a tub when I knew I was being waited on and I jumped into the steam shower, permitting the hot water to wipe away the grime of the past few days.

I was afraid to look down as if there would be a trail of dark evidence spilling down the drain. I hoped it wouldn't stain the virginal tiles at my feet but I knew I was being ridiculous. Showers were meant to withstand grime.

Even without the tub, the steam shower was proving to be hypnotic, the endless supply of hot water washing over my aching muscles lulling me into a near hypnosis until it suddenly became too warm to bear.

Reluctantly, I stepped from the spacious glass box and enveloped myself in a fluffy, white towel, cringing when I saw the color of the linen.

I really hoped I had scrubbed sufficiently. I felt like Elsa had brought home a stray dog to her dollhouse.

Inside the bedroom, Elsa had laid out three different outfits for me to choose from and I had to giggle.

Same old Elsa, I thought, my previously dismal mood evaporating as I selected a simple white bikini and red sundress.

I couldn't believe that childbirth had not altered her figure in the least, the sizes of the clothes exactly the same as they had been in high school.

I dug out some mascara and lip gloss from my purse and ran a brush through my tangled mop of hair but I didn't provide much of an effort. Who was I trying to impress anyway?

I was sure that Elsa's friends were lovely people but they were not the governor and I had no desire or energy to put on airs for them.

Semi-satisfied with my appearance, I ventured out of the beautiful guest room suite toward the center of the house where we had entered and prayed I didn't get lost.

As I neared what I thought was the front door, I heard a low, mellifluous voice pipe toward me through the hall. It was almost as if I was in the steam shower again, his mere words having a near-hypnotic effect on me.

"...something else, I'll tell you," he said and his tone affected me in the strangest way, sending shivers through my body in droves. It was just like hearing a song that touched your heart in an indescribable way, causing goosebumps.

"Anyway, I was just driving past and I thought, shit, I haven't seen Jake in a spell. Thought I'd pop in and say hi."

"Hey, you know I'm glad you're here, buddy but – " Jake replied and I could hear the discomfort in his voice as I approached, a shiver of anticipation flowing through me. Who did that voice belong to?

"Yeah, I know. Elsa will kill you," the stranger interjected, laughing shortly.

"No, it's not that," Jake protested. "Her best friend just moved back home and we're having a welcome home party for her. Elsa told me she's already put off that there are people here. Adding another guest might send them both over the edge. Especially Elsa. Although Gen has a nasty temper too."

I could almost hear the shudder in his voice and it was all I could to do keep from laughing aloud.

"I don't mind one more," I offered, stepping into the front hall but the words almost caught in my throat as my eyes fell on him.

"Gen! You're here!" Jake called jovially, reaching out to embrace me in a hug but for a second, I was frozen in place, unblinking, unmoving.

As my best friend's husband swept me into his huge arms, my eyes were transfixed on Jake's friend.

Our gazes locked and I felt like he was staring directly into the depth of my soul as a half-smile formed on his sulky mouth.

His skin was sun-kissed, just like the sandy blonde of his hair but there was nothing pretty about him. He was one hundred percent man from head to toe.

Perhaps it was the tattoos littering his arms, a

ladder rising up the side of his neck to disappear behind his head, hidden behind the length of his straight hair.

Maybe it was the all-black attire or the way his intense eyes continued to follow me as if he could see right through the peasant-style sundress.

And it didn't bother me in the least. I rather wished he could and that he liked what he saw.

"I – you look great," I told Jake when he released me. "Thank you for letting me borrow your wife to help with my move today."

It took everything in my power to pull my eyes away from the green-eyed hottie standing five feet away.

"As if she was doing you a favor," Jake joked. "She couldn't wait to get out of here and leave me with the two-year-old in potty-training stages."

I laughed.

"I can't wait to meet Cath. I'm so happy for you both," I told him sincerely. Jake beamed while the stranger cleared his throat.

Jake looked up and slapped his palm to his forehead.

"Oh, where are my manners. Jude LaCroix, this is Geneva Rousseau."

"Nice to meet you," I said, extending my hand. He took it, holding it longer than necessary and Jake cleared his throat uncomfortably until Jude released me. I could still feel the aftermath of his touch on my skin, tingling.

"Jude was just leaving," Jake offered but I shook my head vehemently.

"I don't know what Elsa told you," I said quickly. "And I probably came across as a mega-bitch but that's just my nerves. I'm happy to be here and I'm looking forward to the party and to the ribs."

"See? Geneva doesn't mind." He flashed us both a smile that was slightly crooked but devastatingly charming as a result. I wanted to run my tongue over his partially protruding eyetooth and see if it was as sharp as it looked.

"Uh...okay," Jake said slowly but Jude was already extending his arm toward me. I accepted it easily and allowed myself to be led in the other direction from which I had come, toward the back of the house.

The energy surging between us was unmistakable and by the time we had entered the yard, I had forsaken any dismal thought I'd had on arrival.

It was going to be a good night after all.

3

JUDE

It was hard not to notice the look of venom emanating from Elsa Henderson as I led her best friend into the yard but the impact was much diminished by the sexiness radiating from Geneva Rousseau.

The nastiness of Elsa's demeanor was canceled out by magic as if Geneva cast a protective shield around us both.

How the hell has this one been kept a secret from me for so long? I wondered but it wasn't really a mystery. Elsa loathed me after all. She wasn't about to give me the names and descriptions of her friends.

Hell, if I'd had any idea she had one that looked like

this, I would have been on her like a dog on a bone for more information.

Jake and I had known each other since childhood and while we weren't the best of friends, he could certainly tolerate me better than his uptight wife.

Jake was a salt of the earth man, hardworking and level headed but his wife was a stuck-up blue blood, apt to look down her ski-jump nose at anyone with less than a seven-figure income.

But her friend? Well, she seemed just as charmed by me as I was by her.

Some people just have inherently good taste.

"So you're from around here?" I asked, directing her through the French doors to where the rest of the guests had congregated. "How come I haven't seen you before?"

She peered at me as if weighing my question and I noted that she didn't pay attention to any of the curious onlookers who had fully turned their heads to check her out.

It was like no one else was there but her and I.

"Would you have remembered me if you had?"

she asked, a teasing lilt to her voice and I felt a rush of heat through my entire body.

I marveled at the fate that had brought me to the Henderson's that night. After what had happened with Kristy, I had to drive around for a while, letting off steam. And that was how I had ended up here.

Meeting Geneva had to be destiny, the universe's way of showing me that I was not resigned to settling down with a nutcase like Kristy, no matter what she thought about it.

"I would definitely remember you if I had seen you before," I assured her, again catching the shine of her dark eyes.

The afternoon sun was fading away the pale twilight was flattering to her olive complexion and smoldering darkness.

"I grew up in New Orleans," Geneva told me. "But my family has a trailer in Elizabeth. I'm staying there for a while."

"A trailer?" I echoed and her brow furrowed. "In Elizabeth?"

"You sound like a parrot. A judgmental one."

I laughed and shook my head vehemently.

"Not in the least," I assured her. "I just would never envision a friend of Elsa's living in a trailer."

She seemed confused by the comment but before we could continue our chat, a shadow fell over up both.

"Jude. I had no idea you were going to be here."

"Speak of the devil," I mumbled. "Literally."

The ice in Elsa's tone should have frozen me to death but I was used to it. She had never really forgiven me for the time that I'd taken Jake on a camping trip and we ended up getting arrested at a strip club in Baton Rouge.

It had all been a misunderstanding, of course, but Elsa was not the type to listen to reason. All she had deduced was that I had corrupted her husband by bringing Jake to a titty bar.

"I don't think you were on the guest list," Elsa said through clenched teeth.

"And I thought that was just an oversight," I quipped, rather enjoying watching the steam emanate from Elsa's noble little nose.

"I kind of invited him," Geneva offered, laughing slightly. Elsa's blue eyes became slits and I would have bet good money that she could barely see through them.

"There are some people I'd like to introduce you to," Elsa said, moving to take the brunette's arm but Geneva didn't seem to notice her friend's annoyance.

"I'm actually just perfect right here," she replied, shooting the blonde a broad grin. I thought the smoke was about to start billowing from her ears and I wisely guided Geneva toward the refreshment table.

"Suit yourself!"

Elsa stormed off and Geneva stared after her, shock coloring her expression.

"What was that all about?" she asked, blinking in confusion. "I've never seen her so pissed."

"Never mind. I can introduce you to some people," I offered, winking as I reached for a beer from one of the open coolers. "You want one?"

She shook her head in response to the beer.

"I'm not much of a drinker," she confessed and I snorted.

"Is that funny?"

"No, but you must know that if you're gonna last in a small town Louisiana, you're gonna need a hobby. Most people take up drinking."

She giggled.

"I'll keep that in mind."

"So why would you trade up the big city of Nola for nowhere?"

Her coffee eyes were scanning the yard, presumably taking in the detailed landscaping. I had to admit, Jake had a gorgeous home, one he treated with pride and care.

Maybe I'll have a place like this one day too, I thought, an unexpected jolt of envy touching me as I noted the look on her face. But what was I jealous of? Certainly not Jake's life – I couldn't imagine sitting through dinner with Elsa, let alone marrying her.

"I – I didn't leave Nola. I left Nashville and came here," she explained in a rushed breath and suddenly her entire demeanor seemed to shift as she made the revelation.

Her back turned so I was staring at the olive tone of her shoulder, the top of a luscious breast

50

just visible under her dark, cascading waves. Her back seemed to have tensed, causing her to stand taller than her five-foot-five frame.

"Hey," I said, unsure of what happened. "Was it something I said?"

She glanced at me over her shoulder and shook her head quickly, forcing a fake smile on her lips.

"No," she replied. "I'm just really tired. I drove in today and unpacked…it's just been a long day."

I had no way of knowing if she was being truthful or not but I had a strong suspicion there was more than she was offering up.

"Heya, shithead. You crashin' parties now? Ain'tcha done enough damage in this town?"

A chubby brunette with an impish dimple in her right cheek approached and I cringed. How had I not seen her earlier?

"Hey Marybeth," I sighed.

I probably should have left when I had the chance. Things were going to get ugly.

"You're hoggin' all the attention as always? Heya

baby. I'm Marybeth Milner. I'm a good friend of Elsa's."

She stuck a meaty paw at Geneva and the newcomer accepted it.

"Hey. Nice to meet you," Geneva said, pumping her hand. "Elsa's mentioned you. She says you're the den mother."

"I'm that and then some, baby."

Marybeth gave me a meaningful look which told me that my connection with Geneva was about to be broken.

"Come with me, honey. You don't wanna get yourself a rep hanging out with this one. He's gone through so many belts, he keeps the men's store in business," Marybeth instructed, steering Geneva away from me before I could interject.

"Belts?"

Geneva cast me a confused look over her shoulder but I felt my eyes drop as I heard Marybeth's answer.

"Yeah, baby. With all them notches, the leather gets ruined, you know?"

I watched them walk away, my hands becoming fists as they always did when the busybodies got involved.

Fuck. This town is just too damned small. This would never happen in New York. No one would give a fuck who I bang in a big city.

I was stuck, debating what to do as I seethed. I didn't want to walk away from Geneva. I felt like she had some spell on me and I would sit there waiting for her as long as it took her to come back. On the other hand, she might never come back with the likes of Marybeth in her ear.

I didn't have to waste much time deciding.

"What the hell are you doing here, Jude? Did you smell fresh meat or did someone tell you my friend was coming?"

Elsa's eyes were flashing laser beams at me. I guess she had just waited to corner me away from her friend who apparently had no clue about the ice blonde's dark side.

"I smelled burgers," I offered lightly. "Stayed for dessert."

"You will stay the hell away from Geneva. She doesn't need the likes of you in her life."

The likes of me. What did that even mean? They acted like I was some predator who ran around bedding virgins and plundering villages.

In New York, I'd be considered a hot-blooded, American man. Here, I'm some social pariah.

"She looks like she can take care of herself, Elsa," I told her, trying to keep the anger from my tone. I didn't want to get kicked out of the party before at least getting Geneva's number but checking my temper among the clucking hens was proving to be very trying.

"She can take care of herself," Elsa replied coldly. "Much better than you ever will. Did you know that she had a record deal in Nashville?"

I felt the hairs on the back of my neck rise. Was she baiting me or was this real?

"You can check her out on YouTube," Elsa laughed. "She's a musician, a singer. A real singer, Jude, not just some pretender who plucks away at his guitar and hopes that the heavens will part and EMI Records will smile on him. She's ambitious and smart. Most of all, she's too good for you."

Elsa whirled, leaving that slap in my face to sting me to the core of my soul. I realized my mouth was open as I stared after her, my heart thudding.

She's such a bitch. And she's probably full of shit.

I ducked away from the party and retreated into the house, pulling my cell out the breast pocket of my plaid shirt.

I had to see if Elsa was lying to me.

Pulling up YouTube, I searched for her name.

Geneva...Rousseau. There we go.

Almost instantly, I found her and my heart stopped thudding inside my ribcage as her voice piped up from the screen in a sweet, melodic country song. It filled my soul with melancholy and sadness, dredging up emotions I never knew I had.

Slumping against the wall, I felt myself growing lightheaded as she belted out the tune, her fingers trailing over the strings of her guitar flawlessly, her eyes closed and she pitched the ending notes before the screen faded to black.

"Did Elsa tell you about that or were you cyber stalking me?"

I raised my head and stared at Geneva as she slowly approached, her face twisted into a grimace.

"Elsa told me but why didn't you tell me? You're incredible!"

She shrugged and turned her head away as if she didn't want me to see the pink tinge on her face.

"I gave it up."

"You gave up singing?"

"For now, yes."

"What?" I choked. "Why? You're amazing! Your voice! Your songs! Are they your songs?"

"You only heard one," she laughed, tossing her waves over her shoulder. "And yes, I write them."

I stepped toward her, staring down at her, shaking my head in disbelief.

"Elsa said you have a record deal. What happened?"

She shook her head quickly.

"I had a record deal," she corrected. "I – it doesn't exist anymore."

"But if you got one, you can get another one!" I said, my voice charged with excitement.

"I really don't feel like talking about it," she sighed, turning away as if she wished she hadn't made her presence known.

"Wait, Geneva."

I grabbed her arm and she turned back toward me, her eyes wide and filled with something I couldn't identify.

"I should get back to the party," she mumbled but I could see she didn't even believe the words coming out of her mouth.

"Yeah?" I asked without removing my hand from her upper arm, our eyes locked. She didn't fight me and I felt her breaths quicken as she subtly moved her face closer, daring me to make the first move.

Marybeth and Elsa had warned her about me and she still wanted to kiss me.

God damn it. It was too much. She was beautiful and sultry and her voice just aroused and crushed me simultaneously.

I'd be a complete fool to let her go and I wouldn't no matter what the light of day would bring.

"What are you waiting for?" she challenged me, licking her full lips tauntingly and looking at me with those seductive eyes. "I thought you were some great Casanova."

Fuck, how could I say no to that?

4
GENEVA

I'm not entirely sure how we made it back to the pristine white room where I'd showered but as the door closed behind us, I had to shadow thoughts while my fingers twined into his silky blonde tresses.

The first was, if we were caught, Elsa was going to be furious.

The second was, that cream-colored room was not going to seem quite so pure by the time we were finished with it.

But the notions were so far removed from the reality of what was happening, they may not have even come from my own mind.

I was far too caught up in the emotion of what was happening, the shivers of pleasure shooting through my spine like electroshock treatment to my body.

The attraction we had superseded a man and a woman eyeing one another at a party. There was something intangible at work there, as if the fates had intervened and were guiding us toward that glorious canopied bed.

Jude's lips crushed into my throat, his tongue jutting out as he suctioned against the prickled skin, pushing me back onto the thick comforter.

My legs rose, the skirt of the sundress falling over my hips, only the thin material of the bikini and his jeans between us.

I could feel his pulsating hardness grinding against my already moist cleft and I bucked upward, wrapping my thighs around his hips, locking my ankles around his waist.

"You taste so sweet," Jude murmured, his hypnotic voice driving me higher into a state of pleasure as his head dipped lower across my chest. If his breaths were hot, his tongue was scalding and he slowly traced the lines of my cleavage with skillful movements.

I moaned softly when my puckered nipple

found its way into his demanding mouth and I arched my back again, wanting him on all parts of me at once.

Yanking him closer, I allowed my fingertips to trail over the lines of his shoulders, pulling up his faded black Nirvana shirt.

A moan escaped my lips when I saw a mass of rippling muscles. I would have never guessed he was so toned by his seemingly lean frame but the realization only made me wetter and I groaned loudly when his teeth nipped against my flesh.

A bolt of shivers coursed through me and I managed to wrest his top over his head, our eyes locking in a clash of brown and greens as a slow smile formed on his mouth.

"Kiss me," I breathed, wanting to taste his lips again and his beam widened.

"I intend to," he replied, his fingers sliding off my panties as he spoke. Our gazes never wavered until his fingers slid through the sopping cleft of my center.

"Oh shit," I purred, curving my neck to the side as my ass moved up toward him. His head disappeared between my legs and the kisses resumed, soft and burning around the skin of my longing core.

When the first lap of his tongue met throbbing clit, I cried out, not because I wasn't expecting it but because he hit the precise spot he was meant to touch.

"Shh," he muttered, his mouth still pressed against my dripping lips. "I don't want this to get cut short."

Obediently I clamped my mouth shut, reaching my arms above my head for a pillow for which to muffle my sighs of pleasure. He was right; there was no way I wanted our tryst to be interrupted.

Still, I couldn't rush the sensations flooding my trembling body. Each swipe of his tongue against me brought me closer to the climax mounting in the depth of me.

His large hands cupped my cheeks, raising me deeper into his face and I felt beads of sweat forming on my forehead.

"Oh god, yes. Please. More," I whispered breathlessly.

I was going to cum and he sensed it, spreading

my ass apart to toy with my entrance. I howled into the pillow, bucking upward uncontrollably as I spilled forward in hot streams of ecstasy. He was ready for me, lapping each drop with his coarse organ until I felt a second climax following.

But he didn't let me complete my double orgasm, and suddenly, I was on my stomach, legs spread wide as he mounted me from behind.

Jude's breaths were short gasps and a long, pleasured moan emanated from his lips as he plunged into me without warning.

Instantly, the muscles of my center clenched around him, drawing his massive cock into me like a vacuum.

I couldn't suppress the scream as he filled me with more intensity than I'd ever been taken in my life.

My breaths couldn't be caught as his fingers closed into my hips, guiding me higher against his washboard abs, his sack spanking me against my swollen button as I struggled to keep myself on my shaking arms.

But he didn't want me on all fours and his

fingers swept into my hair, twisting my chestnut waves into a knot as he pressed me into the covers.

I let my arms fall, inhaling the material but not noticing the scent of lilacs in the sheets.

All I was aware of was the feeling of Jude's massive cock filling me harder and faster, slipping and sliding. That second orgasm was nigh and I couldn't take it for another second.

"Fuck!" I bellowed, clenching my cheeks against his thrusting shaft, pushing myself so that I felt he had become a part of me, our sweating, shaking bodies becoming one.

He grunted and his muscled form tensed. In seconds, his hot seed was pouring into me like I was a glass for his pitcher of passion.

Again, I squeezed against him, not wanting to lose a second of his release and he held fast to me as his moans lessened and his body slowly relaxed against me.

An unexpected shiver coursed through me and another round of gooseflesh covered me but all the tenseness in me dissipated into a puddle and evaporated from the room as if it had never been there.

"Wow," Jude laughed, falling out of me to lie at my side, his emerald eyes fixated on the ceiling. "That was fun."

I snickered at his characterization.

I bet he said that to all the girls.

"Yeah," I replied. "It was *all right*."

He turned his head to look at me, his eyes still bright with desire, and he leaned forward to pressed a gentle kiss to my lips.

I hadn't been expecting it.

Honestly, I didn't expect to hook up with some stranger at a party my best friend had thrown in my honor. A stranger whom I knew Elsa and the others didn't even want there.

A flash of guilt hit my stomach and I pulled away, sitting up to straighten myself out. This was wrong. I was already falling back into my old patterns, being a rebel without a cause. Was I acting out for shock value or a reaction or... what? Attention?

Shit, what have I done?

I reasoned that a one-night stand was not going to make or break me but I wondered if I hadn't just pursued it because of Jude's kind words about my singing.

It didn't matter; it wasn't going to happen again. It was a one-off.

"What's wrong?" he asked, sounding hurt that I was already on my feet. I ran a hand through my tresses and offered him a tight smile.

"Nothing," I lied. "But we should get back to the party before they dig the pitchforks out of the cabana."

Jude snorted and ambled to his feet also, snatching his pants off the floor.

"Oh well, I should probably get the fuck out of here before that stake gets warmed up. I'm sure Elsa's been adding logs to the fire since she first saw me here."

We grinned at one another.

"Well...maybe I'll see you around town," I told him, unsure of what else to say.

He grabbed my hand before I could reach the door handles and spun me back as if we were in the middle of a salsa dance.

I laughed as he brought his face inches to mine, a lazy smile forming on his face.

"You'll be seeing me around," he agreed, his eyes boring into mine. I couldn't believe that he was still giving me shivers. Maybe it was going to take another round before I got him out of my system.

"Actually, there's an open mic in Alexandria on Thursday nights. You should come. With me." he offered.

I laughed again.

"Yeah, I don't know about that," I replied, gently and reluctantly removing my arm from his grasp. Truthfully, I could feel the heat building in my crotch again and I worried if I didn't move then, we were definitely going to get caught because I was ready to go for another round.

Why did that excite me more?

"The place is called JoJo's," he continued as if I hadn't refused. "I can pick you up if you want."

I smirked and opened the door to the bedroom. Instantly my smile faded as Elsa glared at us like a pissed off rattlesnake.

It was me who recoiled.

"Really?" she barked but she was talking to Jude, not me. "You really went there after our talk?"

Oh shit. What talk?

Jude slipped past us, a bemused expression on his face but I could still smell the telltale scent of sex in the air.

There will be no lying my way out of this one, I thought, slightly embarrassed at being caught. I wasn't sure which was more humiliating; being caught having sex in her house or who I had been having sex with.

I guess both had a part to play in my shame.

"I think this is my cue to leave," he quipped lightly, bowing formally and sarcastically as he ducked out.

Elsa spun to look at me.

"Please tell me you didn't do what I think you did," she sighed, disappointment clouding her blue eyes.

"What do you mean?" I asked innocently, starting back toward the party, my cheeks flushed as she followed me.

"Gen, you're a grown-ass woman and I'm the last person to tell you what to do – even if you are under my roof."

I bristled at the not-so-subtle reminder but I held my tongue. It wasn't a power play. It was just Elsa being Elsa.

"But Jude is bad news," Elsa insisted, joining my side. "I'm not blowing hot air. You can ask anyone."

"What's so bad about him? He's had a few lovers? Who hasn't?"

I eyed the blonde perfectionist, trying to remember how many men she'd been with before marrying Jake and suddenly I felt like a whore.

Most of us have had a few lovers. No one else in the world is as pure as Elsa.

Curiosity had gotten the better of me. It had to be more than the fact he was just a playboy. We had known our fair share of Lotharios and I'd never seen Elsa so hell-bent on keeping me away from a man in my life.

"He's a nobody," she grumbled. "He has no ambition, no drive. He's what you left here to escape and he'll just suck you back in. I could kill Jake for letting him stay."

Inexplicably, I felt a shock of defensiveness.

"That's hardly a fair thing to say, Else. Everyone finds their groove at different times. Just because we happened to get what we wanted early, doesn't mean he's a lost cause."

She sighed and stopped walking.

"I know you're having second thoughts about your career and everything right now, Gen, but don't get dragged into Jude LaCroix's bullshit. He has a girlfriend he's been stringing along for years, refusing to commit. He sits around and strums his guitar because it gets all the local girls hot for him but he's a bum. Trust me. I've known him for years."

She stared at me, her face softening.

"Like I said, I know you're a grown woman but I also know you're vulnerable – "

"I am not vulnerable," I snapped. "I've always taken care of myself and one muscle-laden player is not going to change that. Have a little faith in me."

She chuckled mirthlessly.

"I have all the faith in you," she replied shortly. "It's Jude whom I have absolutely none."

"God, you are such a mother. Save this protectiveness for Cath and don't worry about me."

She didn't respond but her lips were pursed so finely, I almost couldn't see them.

As we returned to the party, I realized I was bothered what she'd said for more than one reason.

Had I just slept with a guy who has a girlfriend?

The idea made me sick to my stomach, given the fact that my daddy had been unable to keep it in his pants while married to my mama.

I had always vowed never to be the "other woman."

I swallowed the sick twisting in my gut.

If what Elsa was saying was true, I definitely had to stay away from Jude. But why did I feel like it was going to be so much harder than I was letting on?

5

JUDE

It was probably a bad idea but I couldn't help myself. The alternative was asking Jake but that would likely mean he'd tell his wife and she'd warn Geneva I was coming.

There was no fucking way I was letting that happen.

Fuck no, I had to do it this way, even if I came across as somewhat stalkerish for it.

I'd parked at the mouth of Little Piney RV Park and waited for some sign of the girl who had been on my mind endlessly for the past four days.

I wished I'd gotten her number but a part of me wondered if she would have given it to me. She seemed determined to leave what had happened between us behind the walls of the bedroom.

It was strange to have the shoe on the other foot for once. Hell, I couldn't remember the last time I'd had to chase a girl. Probably not since elementary school and even then, I can't say I recall a specific incident.

The women had always flocked to me, cooing over my dark lashes and fawning over the green of my eyes.

I was brought lunch and given shoulder rubs, just to play a song or two. I'd never had to court; I'd always been the courted.

But Geneva was not just any woman; she was everything I'd been looking for and not just because of her stunning attractiveness.

I had not been able to stop playing her songs on loop until I had memorized the lyrics to every one I could find.

Damn, I couldn't get enough of her voice, of her soulful eyes and her heartfelt words.

She pierced me as so few musicians had but I knew I couldn't just walk away from her.

I needed to know why she had given it all up. I

needed to know how she found her inspiration. God damn it, I just needed to see her again.

For two hours, I'd been sitting in my truck and I wished I hadn't drunk that last Red Bull. I was going to need to find a washroom soon but I still had no idea which trailer hers was. I'd tried asking a couple of the residents but they were old and surly with no desire to help me whatsoever.

I was just about ready to give up when the door to the last structure opened and my heart skipped like I was some twelve-year-old in puppy love.

Without thinking about what I was going to say, I leaped from the cab and hurried toward her as she locked the door.

"Hey."

She spun, obviously startled by my abrupt arrival.

Her eyes narrowed but not before I saw a spark of interest light them.

"Jude! What are you doing here?"

"Honestly, I really need to use your washroom," I told her truthfully and she eyed me skeptically, unmoving as if she was trying to measure the danger my presence might present.

"They don't have bathrooms in Oakdale?"

"They do," I replied, suddenly very uncomfortable as I shifted my weight from one foot to another. "But I'm currently standing outside your place and Oakdale is fifteen minutes from here."

She continued to stare at me suspiciously but she unlocked the door and let me push my way inside.

It didn't take much to find the toilet and a moment later, I was back in the living room area where she stared at me with her arms crossed over her chest.

"Are you stalking me?" she asked. "This is kinda weird, Jude."

"I'm not stalking you," I promised but I suddenly saw precisely how weird it was. "Listen, I really wanted to see you again."

"Have you ever heard of a phone? Or email? I think I might even feel better about online trolling than this right now."

"I have but you didn't give me your number," I

reminded her. "And I had a feeling that Elsa wasn't about to hand over your calling card any time soon. I really wanted to see you, face-to-face, not be your Facebook friend."

Her arms remained firmly in place.

"Jude, I already told you – that was a onetime thing. And I had no idea you had a girlfriend. I'm a little pissed you didn't mention it, actually."

I blinked and stared at her blankly, my mind spinning at her words.

"I don't have a girlfriend," I replied, wondering what horseshit Elsa and the others were feeding her. "I swear to God, I don't."

"Oh."

A look of relief crossed her face before she could hide it and I felt a flash of victory.

That's one obstacle overcome, I mused. *If those bitches are going to sabotage, they're going to have to do better than that.*

"I can go if you want," I told her, stepping toward her. "Or we can go to that open mic I was telling you about."

She didn't shy away from me, which I took as a good sign and I brushed a strand of hair out of her face as I peered down at her. Her brow knit slightly.

"Yeah, I don't know. I was just going into town for some supplies," she replied but I could hear the uncertainty in her voice. She wanted to say yes.

"We can stop on the way back. I know a twenty-four-hour grocery in Alexandria," I promised. "I also know a place which makes the best jambalaya this side of Nola. We can stop on the way."

"Jude, I don't know…" she said again but any resolve she seemed to have was disappearing with each word she spoke.

"How can you say no to jambalaya?" I insisted. "Are you sure you're a Louisiana girl?"

She sighed and hung her head as if I had defeated her.

"Food sounds good, but I'm not sure about the open mic."

I got it. She wasn't fighting a date with me; she was fighting the idea of getting up on stage.

"Fine," I relented. "We'll go and if you hate it, we'll get the hell outta there. Deal? No pressure, no commitments."

She bit on her lower lip but I knew the cat was in the bag. She had decided from the minute I had told her I was single.

"What do you say?" I urged, wanting her to say it aloud.

"On one condition."

"Anything."

"You can't tell people what you know about me."

I cocked my head to the side and studied her face pensively. Why was it such a secret? What didn't I know?

I was determined to find out.

"I promise."

"Now tell me, how good is this jambalaya?" she asked and I chuckled.

"You'll be thanking me for days," I vowed but it wasn't the food I foresaw her being grateful for.

She was impressed with the jambalaya and I tried to remember the last time I'd eaten at the little shack off route 165, just outside Glenmora.

Once upon a time, I had stopped there every week on my way to the bar to perform on Thursday nights but it had been a long time since I'd had the motivation to go.

Life had been sucking the will to live out of me and maybe I'd given up on the music more than I'd realized.

I hadn't gone to the open mic in at least a year and I wasn't even sure it was still being hosted at JoJo's anymore. Fuck. I really should have researched it online before making such a grand gesture toward Geneva. I really hoped it did because I'd been working on a song for Geneva for the last three days and I wanted to play it for her.

"I should warn you," I told her. "There will be very little talent in that room, myself included."

She cast me a sidelong look as we drove, steering onto I-49 into the heart of Alexandria.

"Are you fishing for compliments before I've

even heard you play?" she asked bluntly and I was taken aback by the question.

She really is not like the other women I know, I thought and for a second, I wondered if that was a good or bad thing. I didn't really know how to cope with someone not out to impress me. I figured I better learn quickly.

"I'm just warning you," I replied, shrugging. "You're a professional. You are used to hearing the real thing, not a bunch of drunken yokels."

"You'd be surprised what passes for talent these days," she commented. "Anyway, I'm not a professional. Not anymore."

I swallowed my reluctance to push her and blurted out the question which had been weighing on me since I'd first learned about her.

"Why?"

"Why what?"

"Why aren't you a professional anymore? You are so gifted, Geneva. You had a record deal – "

"You know, for someone who doesn't have my phone number, you ask a lot of questions," she interjected and I could see her shutting down in front of me. "If I wanted you to know, I am quite capable of telling you without prompts."

"You're right," I agreed quickly, not wanting to instigate a fight. The shoe really was on the other foot and it was damned uncomfortable.

"I know."

A long silence ensued and Geneva turned to look out the window into the fading evening light.

I could see she was regretting her decision to come but I felt like anything I'd say to her would only alienate her more so I opted to keep my mouth shut.

I pulled up into the parking lot and exhaled as I recognized some of the vehicles beneath the neon sign of the bar. Something was still happening on Thursday nights, even if it wasn't open mic.

"Hey," I said before she could open the door and she glanced at me, her mouth drooped into an unhappy frown. I didn't want the night to be a bust before it had even gotten going. I needed to say something to her before we got inside.

"What?"

"I brought you here because I thought it was something we both had in common, Gen. I didn't bring you here to upset you. If this is going to cause tension between us, I'd rather do something else."

She seemed surprised and she blinked quickly, studying my face. A sheepish expression crossed over her and she shook her head.

"No," she sighed. "I'm being a brat. I'm overly sensitive about my adventures in Nashville."

She inhaled sharply and sat back in her seat, releasing her hand from the door handle.

"The truth is, I just got burnt out. I worked so hard to get that record deal, jumping through hoops, acting like a trained poodle. I gave up who I was to appease the agents and the publicists, showing them a 'marketable' side of me when all I wanted to do was make music. I just couldn't take it anymore and I snapped."

"What did you do?" I asked, half-shocked by her stupidity, half-awed by her bravery.

"I told them to take the record deal and shove it. I told my agent that I was nobody's monkey and she could go to hell if she wanted to dye my hair blonde and call me 'Juniper Jane.' I'm not a goddamn Marvel superhero. I'm a musician."

I snorted, trying to envision a bleached blonde version of Geneva, cracking gum and sporting glitter eyeshadow. It didn't jive in my head.

"Anyway, making music isn't about record deals and fame," she continued but I would have had to be deaf not to hear the naked wistfulness in her voice. "It's about art and soul and speaking to people so they hear you. Really hear you."

"You shouldn't have to sell out to make music," I agreed. "I don't blame you."

She offered me a wary smile.

"Thanks for saying that. Everyone else thinks I had some sort of nervous breakdown but that wasn't it at all. I just needed to get out of there before I did. Does that make sense?"

"Yeah," I conceded. "It makes a lot of sense. I think you're really courageous for doing that. I think most people just grin and bear it."

"I'm not most people," Geneva sighed.

"I can see that."

"I have no idea why I just burdened you with my crazy."

"Maybe because you can see that I'm your friend," I suggested. "Or maybe you just needed to get it out your system."

Her eyes were glittering in the dark but my eyes were focused on her mouth.

"You're more than a friend, aren't you?"

If anyone else had asked me that on a first date, I probably would have "developed a massive headache" and cut the night short but there was no hesitation when I answered her.

"I think I am."

"Come on. It's getting too heavy in here," Geneva said, turning to let herself out of the car. The emotion in the cab was making her uncomfortable. As she slipped out, I remained sitting in the driver's seat, watching her for a long moment.

I wondered why I wasn't the least bit put off by what was happening between us.

It should have unnerved me but it didn't as if I had somehow found a kindred spirit for the first time in my life.

6

GENEVA

It happened gradually but with a force that smacked me in the face when I bothered to give it any real thought.

The night we went to JoJo's had changed everything between us and not just because we'd come back to my trailer and made love until five a.m., with the memory of the night fueling our passion toward one another.

Despite what he'd said about his lack of talent, Jude's voice had an effect on me that I rarely felt. I should have known it would when his regular speaking tones already caused my body to erupt into a million shivers.

His music was harder than what I sang, his songs filled with anger and desperation where my country tunes were laced with melancholy and nostalgia.

I listened to him pour his heart into the audience through painful lyrics and I wondered where all his angst stemmed from. There had to be a hurt child inside that cocky exterior but I wasn't sure if I wanted to pry it open. I had so much lost girl inside myself. Did I really need someone else's anguish on top of my own?

But it soon became obvious that we didn't have a say in the matter, that we had been brought together by some unseen hand, guided into one another's lives despite the warnings of my new circle.

"I could kill Jake for letting him stay that day," Elsa fumed one day as we walked through Oakdale, pushing Catharine in her stroller. The toddler cooed and pointed out the few items she could identify as we walked and I pretended to be enthralled with her to avoid Elsa's anger.

"Tree!" Cath announced.

"Very good," I encouraged. "Tree!"

"Stop pretending my daughter is the second coming," Elsa snapped at me.

"He's really not that bad," I insisted, wishing she would leave it alone. It had been two weeks since Jude and I hooked up and my best friend showed no signs of letting go of her anger toward him.

"What is the deal between the two of you anyway? He seems to think you're Cruella Deville although I keep telling him you hate dalmatians and you look terrible in polka dots."

It was meant to be a joke but it only seemed to incense her more.

"Isn't that just like Jude? Turning everything around to make someone else look like the bad guy. It's always someone else's fault with that one. He's never to blame for anything."

I sighed, realizing that our argument was going nowhere.

"Elsa, I love you like a sister," I told her sincerely. "But you're acting like my mother. Jude has not shown me anything to give me concern."

"He will, baby," she assured me, her jaw twitching. "Mark my words."

I saw Marybeth and Carrie waving at us from

the patio of the café and ground my teeth together.

"You were wrong about him having a girlfriend," I reminded her. "Maybe you're wrong about more than that."

"He's been leading Kristy McClellan by the nose since they were children. I guarantee you if you ask her, she'll tell you a very different story than whatever crap he's been filling your head with."

"Elsa..."

"What? You don't want to hear it, I know. But Geneva, this wouldn't be the first time I'd warned you and you dismissed me so easily."

I tensed at the reminder but I was permitted a chance to respond as we neared our other friends.

It was strange that I had fallen into the mommy circle but of course, that had been Elsa's doing. After all, she was a mom now and all her friends were too.

If I'd stuck around, I might be one too, I thought but the idea of settling down and raising a gaggle of children was as laughable to me as rebranding myself "Juniper Jane" of country music fame.

"There she is!" Marybeth cooed, swooping in to collect Cath into her arms. "How are ya, my little petunia?"

Cath laughed, reaching up to pinch Marybeth's chubby face and I sullenly sat in a chair, wishing I'd opted out of lunch.

Jude was working and I didn't want to pace around the trailer without him, not when we had started songs together.

The RV had become a mess of sheet music and scrap paper as we tried to create something beautiful. More often than not, our nights were interrupted as we got distracted in each other's embraces, laughing and talking until the wee hours where we would fall into a peaceful sleep in one another's arms.

The music was serving as an aphrodisiac but it was also a muse and after we were spent, more idea flowed onto the pages.

Our styles were so different; melding them together was proving to be a challenge but it was one we were both up for.

I felt inspired for the first time in ages and I could tell that Jude was in the same place. It wasn't difficult to see when a fellow artist was consumed by their passion.

"What are you smirking at?" Carrie demanded, snapping me out of my reverie. "Thinking about banging that heathen you hooked up with?"

"LANGUAGE!" Marybeth and Elsa hissed in unison, glancing at Cath who was, of course, oblivious to the adult conversation around them.

I liked Carrie's no-nonsense approach to life. Of all Elsa's friends, she was probably most like me but I also resented her for thinking she had any say in my life.

I didn't know her and she certainly didn't know me. Whatever their opinion about Jude, she had no right to offer her two cents to me after two weeks of lunches.

"Yep," I replied. "I was thinking about how he bent me over the – "

"GENEVA!" Elsa roared, her face staining crimson and I shrugged.

"You're the ones who are so interested in what's

happening between Jude and me. I don't want to spare you any of the details."

"Oh honey," Marybeth chuckled. "You think you're the first to give us these details on Jude LaCroix? There ain't many in this town who ain't been taken every which way by him."

She was saying it for shock value but it didn't stop me from reacting.

I stood.

"This was a mistake," I snapped. "I'm getting really sick of you telling me about Jude. You don't have to be happy about it but I would rather you keep your comments to yourselves."

"Sit down, Gen," Elsa sighed. "You're right and I'm sorry."

I blinked and stared at her, wondering if she was trying to trick me in some way.

"Sit down. We have no right to comment on your love life and if Jude makes you happy, have at it."

"We're tryin' to be helpful, baby, not bitches," Marybeth added. "We ain't your enemy."

I was reluctant to believe them but I could read

the grudging contrition on their faces and I lowered myself back into my seat.

"Stop bringing up his past," I insisted. "I don't want to hear this every time we go out."

"We will," they chorused and I exhaled slowly.

I should have just yelled at them a week ago, I realized, settling back into the chair.

"Thank you."

There was an uncomfortable silence as they all pretended to look over their menus and I felt like it was my responsibility to change the subject in light of this new truce.

"We got a gig singing together," I offered and all sets of eyes looked at me in shock.

"What?" Elsa choked. "Singing where? I thought you were taking a break from all that, Gen."

How could I expect her to understand? Elsa's idea of art was making a cornucopia on Thanksgiving or wreaths on Christmas. When passion struck, you needed to embrace it. There was no denying that Jude had awoken the sleeping beast within me.

"We got a show on Friday night at JoJo's in Alexandria. We've been going there for open mic nights and the owner really likes us."

"That's great, baby!" Marybeth cooed, clapping her hands together. "We'll get a group sitter and come, won't we, ladies?"

"Yeah, of course!" Carrie agreed quickly, shooting the others a nervous look but I didn't care. The sooner they got used to the idea of Jude and I together, the better. Maybe after they saw the magic between us on stage, they'd be more forgiving.

In any case, I wasn't doing it so much for my benefit as I was Jude's; his voice needed to be heard to an audience. Mine had already been heard – well, as much as I'd allowed it to be anyway.

"Great!" I said, smiling at them. "I'm hoping that this is the first of a regular thing for us."

"You know, Charlie has a friend who owns a bar in Lafayette, I'll call him and see if they're lookin' for talent out that way."

"Really?" I asked dubiously. "You'd do that, Mary?"

The chubby woman shrugged and nodded.

"Why not, baby? I just told ya – I ain't your enemy. Anyway, I heard all your songs. You sing like an angel. You'd be doin' him a favor."

I was touched by the niceness of her words. Frankly, with all the chaos that mine and Jude's pairing seemed to bring, I hadn't been sure that the girls liked me all that much.

"Thank you, Marybeth! I – we would be honored if you could talk to your husband for us. We're just talking about getting out there but I've found that jumping in with both feet is sometimes the best way."

"Don't thank me yet, girl. I ain't promisin' anythin'. If Jude bombs on Friday…"

There it was. At least I knew that they still loathed him but if she could get us booking gigs, why not?

I knew that using my name would book us into shows without a problem. I may not have been famous but I had a YouTube channel and people had heard my name, particularly in country music scenes.

But I didn't want to overshadow Jude's talent by cashing in on mine.

No, I decided. *He'll get by on his own merit. I'm just helping him get there.*

It made me feel good to be working again, even if it wasn't for me, not really. Jude wanted a taste of what it was to be on stage before people who adored him and I was granting him that opportunity.

Who knew? If all went well, maybe we could showcase ourselves as a pair and I could give it another go in the big times?

But I was getting ahead of myself. Way ahead.

I wasn't even sure if I wanted to step foot back into the business yet. I had to take baby steps and ensure I wasn't selling myself out.

No wonder I was always second-guessing myself. I'd been around people making every decision for me for five years.

I had to sit back, take a deep breath and see what happened.

Still, it was exciting to think about, no matter how fresh it all was. No one would try to change my image if my image was already tied into another. Jude and I fit perfectly together, after all. There was no changing that.

"You're grinning again," Carrie commented and my smile widened.

"I have a lot to smile about," I replied, reaching forward to grasp her and Elsa's hands in mine. "You guys, for one."

My gaze flittered around the table to meet their gazes and the warmth I felt reflecting back was almost palpable.

I'd done the right thing coming home. I was sure of it.

7

JUDE

"And I'm lost in you and I'm lost for you," she sang, her dark eyes meeting mine as her manicured nails closed around the microphone. "And I'll never be found without you."

"But I'm here with you just as I always was, but before it didn't do," I joined her, my hands strumming over my guitar. A gorgeous smile touched her mouth and I was temporarily dazzled by the light of the stage, touching her face. She was radiating, glowing as we picked up the tempo of the song, dipping into the chorus. Our tones matched perfectly and she hummed as I belted out the words we'd worked so hard on for weeks.

"Never again," I crooned. "Here forever n-ow, never again, I could never leave you, h-ow?"

"Never again," she added, our eyes still locked. "Here forever n-ow, never again, I could never leave you, h-ow?"

We faded out as the final note fell off the strings and we waited.

There was a brief pause and the room went crazy, hooting and cheering as we turned to look at our audience.

I was sweating like crazy, my white t-shirt clinging to my body and leaving nothing to the imagination as we rose to take a break from our set.

"Thanks everyone!" Geneva called into the mic. "We're just going to get hydrated and we'll be back to finish up your night so get your tomatoes ready."

A swell of appreciative laughter swept through the overflowing bar and we exited through the wings of the stage.

"Holy shit!" I gasped, turning to spin her off her feet with a bear hug. "I have never seen this place so damned busy! Did you have anything to do with this?"

She laughed as I dropped her back on her feet,

the din of the crowd a few feet away meeting our ears.

I could hear the compliments from where we stood in the near darkness and I was shaking.

"I just mentioned to a couple people that we were playing tonight," she replied, looking at me with smiling eyes. "I guess the word spread or it's a major coincidence."

I had a feeling she'd done more than just "mention" it but I didn't care. I was drunk on the success of the evening.

"Come here," I growled, snaking my arm around her neck and drawing her in for a kiss. Our lips met wetly and she gasped, pulling back as I pressed her against the wall of the side stage.

"What are you doing?" she laughed nervously as my hand reached around the back of her skirt and slipped my palm beneath the nylon of her panties.

"What do you think?"

Before she could protest again, I crushed my lips back to hers, watching her eyes widen dramatically as my finger swiped across the cleft of her core.

She tried to gasp but by tongue stopped her, my other hand massaging the base of her neck. My fingers dipped inside her, two sliding inside her already lubricated opening.

"Oh my God!" she hissed as I yanked her head back to explore the curve of her neck. I was dizzy with power at that moment, exhilaration driving me beyond any reason.

"Baby, if we get caught," she mumbled but there was nothing but thick lust in her tone as my fingers continued to work their way in and out of her.

My thumb manipulated her swollen nub and she tried to buck but I had her firmly in place, the adrenaline pumping through me as I pressed my engorged hardness against her naked thigh.

"I'm going to fuck you," I warned her but she lost in her orgasm as she gushed over my fingers, jerking slightly as she came.

I released my hand from her neck and managed to free my shaft from the confines of my jeans, my fingertips still trailing along the sopping juices of her climax.

Yanking one thigh up against my hip, I positioned myself against her, relishing the feel of my head over her smoldering entrance.

She seemed to get a grip on what was happening, her pupils constricting as she opened her mouth to protest, looking over my shoulder as if she expected someone to be standing there.

"Fuck, Jude, what are you – "

She didn't have an opportunity to finish her sentence as I filled her. As always, her closed around me, sucking me in with walls of her center and I groaned loudly.

I was grateful for the noise in the patrons were causing, muffling the sounds of our unified moans and cries.

I knew what we were doing was wrong but I couldn't help myself. I had never wanted Gen as badly as I had at that moment.

She clenched me tighter, my shaft delving into her as she clung to me with brute force. I couldn't contain myself, ravaging her with all the pent-up energy I'd mustered through the past weeks preparing for the show.

Geneva had given me a glimpse of what I'd

always wanted that night and I wanted to show her my appreciation.

"Oh fuck!" she screamed, not bothering to cover her mouth and I felt her splashing over me, encouraging my release at the same time.

My balls tightened instantly and I sighed, pounding her twice more against the wall until I felt the tug of my seed escaping into her in a torrent.

"Oh shit," I muttered, falling out of her as reality finally caught up with me.

I fell back against the wall as Geneva reclaimed her balance, both of us breathing heavily as we scanned the dark wings for signs we had been witnessed.

"I think I'm going to need a drink," Geneva said and I laughed.

"Yeah, me too."

She pulled herself together as I zipped myself up, wiping my gleaming face with my open palms. I could still smell her on me and it was delicious.

∽

"That girl, she likes you."

I choked and spat out my bourbon onto the porch as my head whirled to look at Jimmy who was lounging in the doorway, his arms crossed over his suspenders. He peered at me with bright blue eyes from underneath the visor of a Saint's ballcap.

"What?" I coughed, wiping my mouth. "Who? What girl?"

I looked into the tree line, thinking someone was standing out there but there was no one. Whipping my head back toward him, I stared at him questioningly.

I was stunned that my roommate had instigated a conversation. In two years, I could not remember him approaching me about anything, let alone a conversational matter.

He may have said we needed toilet paper one time.

"That city girl."

"Geneva? Yeah, of course she likes me. She's my girlfriend," I replied, my brow knit into a deeply creased vee. "What about it?"

"You like her?"

I laughed, wondering not for the first time if Jimmy was brain damaged or autistic in some way.

"She's my girlfriend, Jimmy."

He stared at me unblinkingly as if my answer didn't compute.

"Kristy was your girlfriend."

The words annoyed me and I clenched my jaw.

"What the fuck is your point, Jimmy?"

He shrugged as if he really didn't have one and turned around to retreat into the house.

"Jimmy?"

There was no response and he did not come back out but I felt a cold chill run through me. Jimmy was not someone to just blurt out phrases for no reason. What was his purpose in bringing that up?

It shouldn't have bothered me but it did and I started a process of overthinking which did not stop until Geneva pulled up half an hour later.

"Hey, I'm looking for a sexy musician that lives here," she called, jumping out of the new

Chrysler she'd bought. "About six two, blonde? Lots of tattoos?"

"Oh yeah," I chuckled. "That sounds like Jimmy. Let me get him."

She hurried onto the porch and dropped a warm kiss on my lips.

"Did you miss me?" she purred and I nodded as she sat on my lap.

"What kind of question is that?" I replied, stroking her loose tendril of hair. "You're my favorite side chick."

A look of annoyance crossed her face and I realized that whatever her friends were telling her still weighed heavy on her mind.

"Bad joke," I apologized, kissing her again. "Are you hungry?"

"I am and I know just the place to eat."

"Let me grab my wallet," I told her and she slipped off my lap to let me rise. She was gorgeous in a pair of white shorts that accented her burnt honey skin and shiny hair. Every day I saw her, she seemed more beautiful.

"We might need to stop for gas," she told me

through the screen door. She didn't see Jimmy sitting in the front room listening but I did and I cast him a wary look.

He seemed to be following her words carefully and again, I was triggered by alarm. Since when did Jimmy care about anything anyone had to say?

"Why?" I called back. "Where are we going?"

"Lafayette."

I snatched my wallet off the dresser and headed back to the porch where she was grinning like a bird-filled cat.

"What's in Lafayette?"

"Our new gig."

I stared at her.

"We have a gig in Lafayette?" I asked and she nodded, grinning happily. "Every Saturday night. We've gotta sign the papers but it's a six-month commitment to start."

"You're incredible," I murmured, pulling her into me and burying my face in her hair. "How did you do this?"

"I'm just that good," she teased but suddenly, a weird pang of envy shot through me.

Has she been calling in favors for us? Getting in contact with people in Nashville?

Every show at JoJo's had been filled since we'd started doing them and not that I was complaining but I had to wonder if Geneva Rousseau wasn't the reason that the place was always so hopping.

"What's the matter?" she asked, noticing the change in my expression.

"What? Oh nothing, nothing," I replied quickly, grinning at her as we separated. "I'm just thinking that's great news. I can't wait to see this place."

"It's great!" Geneva gushed as we turned away from the cottage toward the car. "It's twice the size of JoJo's and it's newly renovated."

"When were you there?" I demanded, the question coming out harsher than I had intended but she didn't seem to notice.

"Well, I had to check it out. I wasn't going to agree to play in some shithole," she replied easily, not noticing the sudden bite to my voice. I unlocked my truck and let her in the passenger side before ambling toward the driver's side.

A twisty feeling in my gut churned my stomach slightly as something slapped me in the face with full force.

All the time we'd been performing, I'd thought of us as a partnership but the truth was, I was just riding off the coattails of Geneva's success.

The realization made me dizzy.

"Babe? Are you okay? You just went deathly pale!"

I forced myself to be rational, to stop being such a cynic, stop trying to eat away at my own happiness.

But no amount of logic would stop the doubts from swimming through me like a tsunami and for the first time since meeting Geneva, I had a bad feeling about our future together.

8
JUDE

We signed the papers at La Fontaine Crème and started our weekly gigs there but something had changed between us.

I knew it was all on me and I desperately wanted to change the way I felt but there was an animus mounting in me as we performed and Geneva could sense it.

Of course she could. She wasn't stupid and no matter how hard I tried to hide it, I was snapping at her for stupid things and opting out of spending evenings together.

"You're getting sick of this," she commented one night and I glanced away from the TV to look at her.

"It's all right. I've seen it before."

"Not the damned show, Jude, this. Us."

A stab of panic gripped me as I shook my head vehemently.

"No! I'm not!" I protested and it was true. I wasn't ready to call it quits with Geneva, not when she still turned me on more than any other woman I'd ever met. I still thought she was beautiful and her voice, our songs – well, that wasn't something I was going to just throw away.

But I still couldn't shake the resentment I'd been building against her, no matter what I did. And it seemed to be growing, not dwindling as I'd hoped.

"Why are you acting like such an ass the couple weeks? Ever since we took the gig at La Fontaine, you seem more on edge. Is it too much for you?"

Again, I shook my head vehemently.

"No," I insisted but I quickly changed my mind. "Yes, maybe it is."

I had to lie. The truth was too painful to tell her.

Her face softened and she scooted closer to me on the sofa.

"Why didn't you say something?" she demanded. "We'll break the contract and pay the penalty."

"No way!" I almost yelled. "These shows – they're what keeps me going, Gen. But I'm tired, yes. Between work and the rehearsals..."

"I get it," she sighed, flopping back against the cushions and taking my hand. "It's a lot."

I was silent for a minute, weighing the pros and cons of asking the next question on my mind.

It wasn't worth it. She would just take it the wrong way and we'd end up having a fight. I'd been down this road with Kristy too many times.

Gen isn't Kristy, a voice in my head snapped and I immediately silenced it.

"What do you want to do about it?" she asked after a long silence and I snickered.

"I want to get a record deal so I don't have to hang out with dead grandmas all day, picking up their dead flowers."

I felt her tense but I didn't meet her eyes. I wished I could take that back. I knew what was coming and I really wasn't in the mood for it.

"You think that's what you want," she sighed. "But when you get it – "

"Boo hoo, poor talented girl who had to change her hair for a record deal," I yelled, jumping to my feet. I was sick of her pity party, all the stress I'd had building in me beginning to take shape.

I was angry at her, angry for not seeing what she had when it was staring her in the face. Obviously, she'd never been poor or worked a day in her life.

"What did you just say to me?"

The liquid nitrogen in her tone should have told me to stop while I was ahead but I couldn't quit. I had to get it all out.

"Just because you fucked everything up for yourself, Geneva, doesn't mean that I have to. I mean what's the big deal about changing your name? The music would still be yours and – "

"You're a selfish, ignorant ass," she spat, her face inches from mine. "And you don't know a goddamned thing about me. I worked my ass off to get where I was. Walking away from that was the hardest thing I ever had to do so don't pretend you have any idea what's involved when you sit at home in your little cottage, working your safe little job and have never taken a risk a day in your life."

She spun and stormed out of my house, slamming the door so hard, it reverberated the deer head mounted on the wall.

"Fuck!" I yelled, wondering what the hell was wrong with me. "Fuck!"

"I don't think she likes you anymore."

I howled and whipped my head toward Jimmy who smirked at me from the back hallway.

"Fuck you, Jimmy," I growled, stalking out toward the door, throwing it open to peer into the night.

Of course she was gone but I was relieved she was. I wouldn't have known what to say to make it right if she had been there.

Did I even want to make it right?

What kind of dumb ass question is that? Of course you do; this girl is everything to you.

Or was she taking everything from me?

I had to ask myself how many drinks I'd had because I was talking myself in circles and as I stood on the porch, counting mentally, I saw headlights coming back down the road toward my house.

My pulse quickened and I darted down the steps to greet the car as it stopped. The fact I was happy to see her answered all my questions but when I neared the vehicle, I realized it wasn't Gen's car.

"Oh fucking great!" I muttered aloud, freezing in my tracks. Kristy jumped from the driver's side and sauntered toward me.

"Nice to see ya too," she yelled back at me. "Why ain'tcha answerin' your damned texts?"

"I blocked you," I replied truthfully. "On Facebook, Twitter and Instagram too."

"You gotta lot of damn nerve," she snarled. "After what you've done."

I rolled my eyes.

"Can we make this quick, Kristy? I'm really not in the mood tonight."

"I betcha ain't," she retorted, striding closer, her face contorted in anger. "You've been runnin' around with that city girl, pretendin' that you're a rock star."

My eyes narrowed and I felt my mouth purse together. What the fuck did Kristy know about Geneva and what was the crazy bitch going to do about it?

"Does she make you feel special, baby? Like you're doin' somethin' useful for once."

"Go home, Kristy."

I turned away, knowing my temper was about to flare epidemically but she wasn't finished with me yet and she snatched at the back of my shirt.

"I can't. Baby, I'm pregnant," she moaned.

I felt like the outdoors had walls and that those walls were closing in around my head.

"What?" I choked. "You're...what?"

"I'm pregnant! We're gonna have a – "

"Shut up!" I roared, slapping her hand away. "You're a sick bitch, you know that?"

She dug through her purse and thrust a Ziploc

baggie at me but I knew what it was before she handed it to me. I didn't touch it. I couldn't even look at the pregnancy test.

"Jesus Christ, Kristy! You were supposed to be on the pill!" I moaned. "You did this on purpose!"

She gaped at me.

"I should have known that you'd be an ass about this."

"How did you expect me to react?" I screeched. "You expected me to be happy about being trapped into fatherhood?"

She shook her head slowly, eyeing me with disbelief.

"I should have known," she muttered again, turning away, her shoulders sagging dejectedly.

"Wait!" I yelled, striding toward her. "Just wait."

Now what was I going to do? My head was already in chaos, my life on the brink of something actually happening and now the universe throws this in my face?

"What?"

She stared at me with wide blue eyes, willing me to say the right thing.

"We'll figure this out," I promised. "Just go away and I'll call you tomorrow. I can't deal with you – with this – right now."

She cocked her head to the side and for a second I thought she was going to slap me but instead, she threw her arms around my neck and kissed me on the lips.

"I knew I could count on ya, baby!" she howled. I shoved her back gently, the feel of her arms around me causing me to shudder.

It was sickening to imagine anyone else touching me after the connection I'd shared with Geneva but it looked like I wasn't going to have to worry about any of that anymore.

I was going to be the god damned man I'd always sworn I wouldn't be: stuck in Oakdale, raising kids as I mowed lawns for the rest of my life.

"Call me!" Kristy cried, her face bright and cheerful as if she hadn't ruined my life forever but I couldn't bring myself to respond as she got into her still running car and drove away from the cottage.

I stumbled back toward the step and allowed my ass to hit the top step as I buried my face in my hands.

There would be no way out of this. Kristy would never let me off the hook and I would be working triple shifts to support a newborn.

In my pocket, my cell dinged and I reached for it, certain it was Kristy, prepared to drive home her twisted victory.

She had done this on purpose, I was sure. But there was nothing I could do about it now.

Maybe I'm not the father, I thought hopefully but I also knew that Kristy was stupidly devoted to me. If there was another guy, I would have heard about it through the town's incestuous grapevine.

This is my penance. I should never have let her keep coming back when I knew I didn't feel that way about her. Dammit!

I read the text, sliding my phone into the unlock position and my head began to pound. It was from Geneva.

<I just spoke with Jason at the Fontaine. I'm off the contract. It's all yours>

The words drove a stake through my heart and I began to hyperventilate.

How had I managed to make a mess of everything in less than an hour? Before the sun had set, I had been close to the happiest I'd been in my life and suddenly, I was sitting outside, pining for my own death.

<We're a team!> I replied.

<Are we?>

I stared at the message for a long moment, unsure of how to reply.

It was a valid question. I had always thought we were a team. I had thought we were more than a team, a part of one another.

But I couldn't deal with Geneva right now.

Maybe she was right to split us up on the contract at the Fontaine. Maybe we needed some space.

<I love you> I messaged her but after ten minutes, I finally rose and headed back into the house, realizing that there was not a response coming.

"Kristy's back."

I closed the door behind me and looked at my roommate, again stunned at his newfound verbal diarrhea.

"Since when do you speak so much, huh?" I snapped. "And since when do you spy on me?"

Jimmy shrugged nonchalantly and turned his head back toward the television screen where Gen and I had been watching earlier.

"Jimmy?"

He nodded but he didn't look up.

"Why are you asking about Geneva?"

Slowly, he lifted his head and stared at me with bright eyes.

"Because I'm in love with her," he replied simply.

I exhaled in a whoosh of hot air.

That was it. I was done for the night.

9
GENEVA

I didn't tell anyone what was happening with Jude and me. I didn't want to deal with "I told you so" I knew would accompany my venting. That's not really fair; Elsa would never come out and say that but she would be thinking it and that was bad enough.

I stayed in my trailer over the next few days and ignored texts from everyone, knowing that I needed some brooding time.

But on the third day, when Jude didn't come by to check on me, I grew desolate.

How could I not have seen that he resented me? I had gone out of my way to ensure that everything we'd done, we'd done together. I hadn't called anyone from Nashville to let them know I was considering getting back into the scene.

It was just another conversation I didn't want to have.

On Saturday night, I had drunk a six pack of Bud and passed out, the alcohol a somewhat foreign concept to my body.

It wasn't until Jude was in bed next to me that I realized someone was in the trailer.

"Holy shit!" I screamed when he brushed the hair off my face. I swung wildly, contacting his face.

"Woah," he cried, grabbing my wrists. "Relax. It's just me!"

I sat up and stared at his face in the dark, willing myself to breathe normally. I had forgotten I'd given him a key.

I'd have to remember to get it back. Make a clean break.

"What are you doing here, Jude?" I whispered although I had no idea why I was whispering.

He stared at me, a strange expression on his face but he didn't answer right away.

"Did you go to Lafayette?" I asked, shaking my head as if to clear it. I was fuzzy from the beer still and I reached for my phone to look at the time. "Tell me you didn't fuck up and miss the show. Tell me you played tonight."

It was after three in the morning.

"I did and that's why I'm here," he replied softly, sitting back. "I got offered a record deal tonight, Gen."

Inadvertently, I laughed although that was not the reaction I'd meant to have. The combination of surprise and the surreal quality of the conversation made me feel like Alice in Wonderland.

And he's the Mad Hatter.

He didn't appreciate my response either and he scowled.

"Thanks."

"No, babe, I'm sorry," I sighed. "I'm still sleeping. Who offered you a contract? When? Where?"

"At the Fontaine. A Sony exec with too much time on his hands came to see me tonight. He had the paperwork in hand and everything.

Apparently, he's heard us sing together a few times."

I blinked.

"But he only offered you a contract?"

He stared at me and I could see he was trying to be delicate.

"It's not that he didn't like your voice, Gen, it's just – "

"That's great," I said again, my voice like a razor's edge. "I – never mind. What did you say?"

I was swimming in emotions, unsure of how I felt as I watched his face.

"Jude?"

"I said..."

"You signed it without even reading it, didn't you?"

Why was I surprised? I should have known he would do something like that. He was impulsive. Careless. I'd always known that and now he was proving it again.

But he was being groomed by Sony and I was living in a trailer park.

He was getting out of Oakdale and I was staying behind. He was leaving me behind even though I was the one who had brought him up, worked on songs with him, inspired him and gotten him off his ass.

"I need this," he told me pleadingly. "You don't know the entire story but I really need this, Gen."

I scoffed and flopped back onto the bed.

"Well, congrats. Have fun. Can I go back to bed?"

"Gen, you can come with me!"

I sprung back up.

"You're a piece of work, you know that?" I yelled, throwing the blankets aside to get onto my knees and lash out with all the anger I'd been burning. "You expect me to jump because you said so? I told you why I came here. You think just because you and I had some sex that I'm going to drop everything and run to be with you?"

I had no right to act that way but the reason

was the least of my concerns at that moment. I was lashing out in my hurt, in my confusion.

"Gen listen to me – "

"No! You listen to me. We had our fun. Get out and don't come back. Congrats on your contract."

"Gen, you don't mean that."

"I do. I mean that. Everyone was right about you, Jude. You're just a snake charmer. Go enjoy your fame. You deserve it."

My voice was saturated with sarcasm and he caught every drop of it.

"Get out!" I yelled, looking for something to throw at him. "Get out! Get out! Get out!"

He rose from the bed slowly and stared at me as if he was looking at a stranger.

"I really need – "

"Stop fucking talking and get out!"

I settled on a pillow and whipped it at his head. He shook his head, disgust and confusion overwhelming his face.

"Okay," he mumbled. "Okay, fine."

He turned and left me just as I had requested.

You're being nuts. Go after him and apologize for being such a whack job. You should be happy for him. This is what you want for him.

But it wasn't, not in the least.

I wanted him to stay with me and write with me and be with me.

Now he'd be off to LA or New York, whisked off into the life I'd known so well and they would change him just as Nashville had changed me.

It's not too late. It's not too late. Get up and go.

I closed my eyes and turned onto my side, curling the blankets into my stomach and allowed the tears to flow freely down my cheeks.

This was exactly what I didn't need. I didn't need a man ruining my quest for inner peace, questioning my own talent and abilities.

I didn't need someone who would just up and run at the first opportunity, an opportunity that should have been ours.

Well, it could have been yours but Sony didn't want you, remember?

The problem was, I had no idea what I wanted anymore. As I lay, sobbing silently into my pillow, I realized *that* was my problem.

I had never really known what I wanted.

10

GENEVA

I heard a car door outside but I sat, still wrapped in a towel, staring at the ceiling. My hair was almost dry.

They had taken their sweet ass time coming back, hadn't they?

Who could blame them? I didn't want to see what came next either, even though I knew exactly what I was expecting.

Ha! Expecting. Glad I still see the humor in this.

"Baby? You in here?"

"Where else was I gonna be?" I snapped back and Elsa peered at me and then looked around.

"You haven't been drinking anymore since we left, have you?"

I scoffed and flopped sideways onto the sofa, ignoring her question but a thousand stabs of guilt pierced me as I realized what I'd been doing to myself in the past weeks.

Had I done it purposely?

I didn't want to think about it.

"Did you get it?" I demanded.

"It's right here," Carrie said, tossing the CVS bag at me.

I made no move to take it even as the trio stood in a semi-circle around me, waiting for me.

"Okay, thanks. You can go now," I sighed, knowing there was no way they were leaving me.

Carrie snickered and plopped down beside me as if to confirm what I already knew, throwing her feet up on the coffee table and reaching for a discarded guitar magazine. Of course, she had no interest in the content but she made her point clearly; no one was going anywhere until I peed on a stick.

"I'll get you some water," Elsa said, turning for the kitchen but I didn't need it. I grabbed for the bag and was on my feet before she could move.

"Gen – "

"I've got this," I said, slipping into the bathroom and sliding the door shut. There was no sense in prolonging the inevitable. I'd put it off for at least three weeks, ever since I'd first noticed I was late.

I must have been pregnant before he left. That would have explained the mood swings, the need to have him stay and the desire to let him go.

The test was merely a formality. I already knew the truth and now everyone else was going to know it too.

It took no time to do the deed, my bladder cooperating fully with what needed to be done.

All that was left to do was wait.

"Gen?"

Elsa was outside the door and I could hear the concern in her voice.

"What?"

"Can I come in?"

I started to say no but I changed my mind. After all, why not? It was better than being left to my own thoughts as I waited for the sticks to appear.

Sliding open the door, I allowed her to come in and didn't bother closing it again. It didn't matter if the others heard. There were no secrets now.

"You should call him," she told me. "He should be here for this."

I scoffed.

"He made his choice to go," I replied. "I'm not going to be the girl back home who pulls him away from his dream because I got knocked up."

"That's not your decision to make!" she insisted. "You owe it to your baby."

"Hey!" I growled, pulling myself off the toilet. "Listen. All of you."

Tentatively, Marybeth and Carrie appeared outside the door.

"Whatever happens here, this is my choice. Jude already made his when he hopped on that plane to LA. You'll keep quiet about this until I decide what to do. Is that clear?"

They stared at me, unspeaking and my eyes narrowed.

"I'm serious!" I barked. "This is no one's business but mine. This is a stupidly small town and the last thing I want is tongues wagging. You don't get to tell anyone. Not even your husbands."

"Geneva, you gonna need support, honey – "Marybeth started to say.

"If you decide to keep it," Elsa interjected, shooting the chunky brunette a warning look.

"No matter what!" Marybeth insisted. "This ain't somethin' you can do alone, no matter how strong you think you are."

"Not a word!" I insisted. "If you can't promise me that, get out right now."

Their jaws dropped at my harshness but no one made a move to leave.

I exhaled slowly, my shoulders sagging.

Despite the fact they hadn't said anything, I sensed they were on my side.

"It'll be all right, baby," Elsa assured me, pulling me into a hug and to my surprise my arms instinctively wrapped around her.

I hadn't been touched since the night I'd thrown Jude out of the trailer and the feel of her comforting hug around my body almost brought tears to my eyes.

"No matter what, we'll figure this out."

I blinked back the tears in my eyes and nodded, clearing my throat.

"I know," I said, reluctantly pulling back and smiling at her. "I've been in worse situations, haven't I?"

Elsa didn't answer and I could tell she couldn't think of one off the top of her head.

"It's time," she murmured, gesturing toward the sink where I'd left the test.

"You look at it," I sighed. "I don't want to."

"You're a big girl now," Elsa said firmly but I could see she already knew what it said. Gulping back the emotion in my throat I nodded and reached for the stick, inhaling sharply as I looked.

"What does it say?"

Even though I'd been expecting it, the blood still rushed from my face to my feet and I swooned slightly at the sight of the double blue lines.

"Oh honey," someone mumbled but I'm not sure which woman it was. "What are you gonna do?"

I shook my head slowly.

There was only one thing to do, without a question.

I ran my palms across my still-flat stomach and lifted my head toward the women, sorrow coloring my face.

The expression must have told them so much and Marybeth looked away as if she was disgusted by what she saw but my best friend grabbed me by the shoulders and looked me in the eye.

"Whatever you decide," Elsa insisted. "There will be no judgement, no – "

"I'm gonna be a mom," I said and there was a collective gasp. It was not the response they had been expecting.

"Are you sure?" Carrie mumbled, looking at me uncertainly. "Are you going to tell Jude?"

"No," I replied firmly. "I'm not telling Jude and neither are you. As far as anyone will know, this baby could be anyone's. I'm going to Lafayette to be near Marc and you will say nothing until I announce it in a month or so, okay?"

They looked at me dumbly and I could see they didn't agree but slowly, they began to nod, one by one.

"If you're sure this is what you want..." Elsa said dubiously but she knew me well enough to know that once my mind was made up, there was little anyone could say to change it. She didn't know that the "what if" had been weighing heavily in my mind since I'd first missed my period.

A plan was already underway whether I'd been consciously aware of it or not.

"It is."

Elsa sighed heavily.

"All right, baby. We're here for you if you decide to stay."

"I won't," I replied firmly.

I should have gone home to Nola in the first place. Coming here was a mistake but from now on, there's no more room for error, not when a baby is involved. All the screw-ups, the rebellions, the escaping, there's no more room for that. It's bigger than you now. It's all about this peanut growing inside you.

I raised my head and smiled at the women and it was a genuine smile through the sick feeling in my gut.

"I won't change my mind," I said again, my words firm with conviction. "I'm sure about this."

And for once in my life, I meant it.

11

GENEVA

Four Years Later

"Cheyenne, I am not going to tell you again!" I yelled. "Next time, you're gonna get a tap on your rump!"

"Wyatt ain't got on his shoes either!" my daughter protested. "Look!"

"Wyatt," I said between clenched teeth. "You are both trying my patience!"

"Just go," Sara laughed as she entered the kitchen. "You're gonna be late if you try to wrangle these two all day long."

"Emma is expecting them," I protested.

"I can watch them today," she assured me. "Don't worry."

I looked at her gratefully and then at the time on the microwave. My sister-in-law was right. If I wasted one more minute fighting with them, I was going to lose my audition and I couldn't afford it.

"Are you sure?" I asked her but there was no real concern in my voice. I knew my brother's wife was a saint, one who loved my unruly children for some reason I could not entirely fathom.

I mean, I adored them, despite the daily reminder of the man I'd lost, their resemblance uncanny to their father. But they were mine, and I loved them.

Sara's patience with the three-year-old twins was beyond anything I'd ever seen. She was wasting her talents as a housewife, no matter how much money my brother made in real estate. She would be the most sought-after daycare worker in the world if she ventured into childcare.

"No, wait, mama!" Cheyenne shrieked as I grabbed my purse from the counter. "I ain't gonna be long! I come with you!"

I smiled affectionately down at the blonde imp who was my bossy, impossible daughter. Her face was contorted in worry.

"Not today, baby. Mama's got an important interview today. This could change a lot for us if it goes well."

She stared at me with green eyes exactly like Jude's, as if she didn't believe a word that was coming out of my mouth.

"Like what?" she demanded.

"Like we can get our own house," I offered, casting Sara a wry smile.

"Why? We live with Auntie Sara and Uncle Marc," Wyatt piped in, poking his head out from beneath the kitchen table where he was playing with his action figures.

"And we love having you here!" Sara added, looking at me meaningfully. I smiled wryly at them ganging up on me but I knew what needed to be done.

It had been a rocky four years, the moving the trailer from Elizabeth to Lafayette so I could give birth near the only family I had; a brother who was furious with me for being an unwed mother.

"It's a new millennium, Marc," I'd told him. "Having a husband isn't a prerequisite for having babies."

"Babies! Twins! How the hell are you going to sustain yourself?"

"She can stay with us when the twins are born," Sara interjected in her calm way. "It will be nice to have little ones running around."

There had been a wistfulness in her tone and it only fueled my guilt, knowing that Sara was unable to have children of her own.

"Just until I get on my feet again," I promised.

"Who is this bastard who knocked you up?" my brother insisted but I never told him. Jude existed a lifetime ago. He was Judas Crowe now, the lead singer in a hot, multi-platinum band. The country boy I'd known, the man I'd shared those forbidden passions with was not the same person.

But then again, I wasn't the same girl either, was I?

According to Elsa, he had not returned to

Oakdale once since signing to the label. I'd long since gotten rid of my old phone so I had no way of knowing if he'd ever reached out to me but I didn't care.

He was a distant memory, not the father of my kids. He'd made his choice and I'd made mine.

I'd stayed in the trailer until I was in my eighth month, my pregnancy going surprisingly well and the twins were born full term at thirty-eight weeks although everyone else believed them early because of the lie I'd told.

If Jude ever did come back and my name was brought up, he'd have no reason to suspect that Chey and Wyatt were his.

Not that he would ask about me. Why should he? He had everything he wanted now. A washed-out singer with babies didn't fit into his life.

"Hurry up, sweetie!" Sara urged. "You're gonna be late!"

I snapped out of my reverie and grinned at them, trying to shove away the shadow of melancholy seizing my heart.

Sara was right; I needed this. We needed this. I

couldn't live with my brother forever and motherhood had changed me.

It didn't matter what I wanted anymore. I had been granted a second chance now, one which I knew not everyone could claim. I would not screw it up this time.

"Mama, please!" Cheyenne called. "Can I come with you?"

Shame swelled in my heart as I opened my arms to allow her and her brother into my embrace.

If this audition panned out, it would open a lot of doors for me, ones which I'd known before, ones which would monopolize my time and take me away from these tiny keepers of my heart.

"Not this time, Chey-Chey," I told her softly, stroking her blonde tresses. "But can you wish mama luck?"

"Good luck!" the twins chorused, pulling back to stare at me with identical green eyes.

"I love you both. Be good for your auntie."

"Okay mama," they agreed and I smiled.

"Thanks, Sara. I'll be home as soon as I can."

"Take your time," she said, ushering me gently

out the door to walk me to the Range Rover parked in the triple driveway. "You've earned a day away from the kids."

I paused to look at her, a slight frown touching my lips.

"If this happens," I told her in a low voice. "It will mean a lot of changes for all of us."

"I know. But if this what you feel you need to do, Gen, you should do it."

I chewed on my lower lip and nodded, unlocking my brother's car with the fob. I had a bit of a drive ahead of me, over two hours to ponder the choice I was about to make.

"Drive safe, ya hear?"

"I hear," I laughed, hopping into the car. "And drop the twins off at Emma's if you have things to do. She doesn't mind."

"I don't mind either," Sara reminded me, waving as I backed out of the driveway. "You make sure you text when you get to Nola!"

"I will," I promised.

I guided the vehicle toward the interstate,

turning on the Sirius radio and settling on an alternative rock station as I drove.

I flipped my head back slightly, catching a flash of my face in the rear-view and I grimaced slightly.

My make-up was perfect, the cat-like curve of my eyeliner accenting my dark eyes exotically beneath a layer of pink eyeshadow. The shade matched my lipstick perfectly and seemed almost offensive against the gleaming dark of my new bob that ended just at my mouth.

I hated my new look. It was not me in the least but that was the point.

The email had been specific – as if spelling it out for an idiot. The colors, the wardrobe, the way I was to wear my hair – all in bullet points.

<This is going to be your last chance, Gen. Don't screw it up> Ashleigh texted. <And if you do, lose my number>

It had taken me two years to get this interview and I had no intention of messing it up, even though it went against everything in me.

Almost five years ago, I ran screaming from all this. And now I was back. After all, I was a mother now, one who had a way to provide for her children so that they would never want for anything again. What was standing in my way?

I'd been living off my brother for years. I couldn't sit around and do nothing. I had no job experience, not when I'd hightailed it to Nashville on my twentieth birthday to follow my calling.

I was an uneducated single mom with one talent, a talent I had stupidly walked away from.

"...new single from No Excuse. Here's 'Leaving to Stay'," the announcer intoned and the twang of an electric guitar filled the car.

A familiar, almost forgotten rash of gooseflesh exploded over my arms as the sound of Jude's voice met my ears.

"I made a mistake," he sang. *"It's been all I can take but you're gone again..."*

Son of a bitch!

My knuckles tightened.

"You begged me to go, but now I know that you wanted me near..."

"You bastard!" I yelled, thumping my fist

against the steering wheel. It was one of our songs, one we had performed together, written together in between bouts of hot sex and cold pizza. I was livid but I couldn't deny that he sang it so well, the hardening of the chords making me feel deeper than I had when we'd sang it.

It wasn't the first time he'd used our songs but usually they had been so massacred, so bastardized, it wasn't the same tune by the time it had been mastered and aired for public consumption.

Not this one. I knew this one. I loved this song. I had poured so much of myself into it and now my part was gone, replaced by a drum solo and spun into a ballad about a bitch who had walked out on him.

Furiously, I poked off the stereo and pressed my foot to the gas as if I could leave the memory of what I'd heard in the distance but of course it was stuck in my head now, a combination of how it had been and what it had been turned into melding together in my mind.

Why does the past keep sneaking up on me when I least expect it?

Isn't it enough that I see him in my kids every single day?

I ground my teeth so hard, I heard a crunch.

But I won't let him resurface now. I was moving forward and doing fine. Jude LaCroix doesn't exist anymore.

Just like Geneva Rousseau was about to disappear. If I played my cards right.

12

JUDE

"Here, baby. That one's for you."

The redheaded girl sat back, rubbing her nose as she snorted back the line, handing me the hundred-dollar bill with her other hand.

I accepted it and leaned forward to take my turn, catching a look at my reflection in the tray where the white powder lay.

I was looking rough and even in the wavering lines of the sterling silver image, I could see the red of my eyes and gauntness in my cheeks.

Hal was going to flip if he saw me like that but I intended to have myself cleaned up before he returned from Japan.

If the rest of the band kept their mouths shut, I'd be fine.

I followed the redhead's lead, inhaling the coke through the bill and flopped back on the oxblood sofa as the sensation of invincibility swept over me.

"I'm gonna order room service," the girl announced, reaching over to grab the menu from an end table but I stopped her.

"No," I told her. "I've got a better idea."

She turned to me, her blue eyes huge as she grinned.

"Oh yeah?" she purred. "Like what?"

"Well," I replied suggestively, lowering her head gently into my lap. "If you open my pants, you might get inspired."

She giggled and fumbled to unzip the faded jeans from around my taut stomach, pausing to trace her fingers over the tiger tattoo, baring its teeth in a ferocious growl.

It had been one of my first and I remembered how strong I'd felt sitting on that chair all those years ago, pretending not to flinch as the needles struck the tender flesh of my abdomen.

"You are so sexy," she sighed, pressing her lips against the image of the tiger. "How are you single?"

Unexpectedly, the question made me defensive and I sat up, pushing her off.

"What?" she asked, her face twisting in confusion. "What's wrong?"

"I'm tired," I snapped irritably. "Time for you to go."

She pouted and righted herself, reaching for the bill to do another line before rising to her feet.

I gazed at her as she collected her purse, watching as she stuffed random belongings into the pouch, a scowl on her face.

"Trevor said you were fun," she muttered and I bristled. "Tell him I said he was wrong."

"Just get out," I snarled and she sashayed around the room deliberately, casting me a baleful look before storming from the suite.

I didn't even know her name but that wasn't uncommon — there were so many groupies coming and going. This one had been hanging around the band ever since we landed in

Toronto. Apparently, our drummer had found her and she hadn't left since our first show.

Suddenly I realized what annoyed me about her.

She reminded me of Kristy.

My buzz was effectively ruined and I rose from the couch, pulling open the double French doors to the balcony overlooking the city, rolling my shoulders and trying to unhinge my locked jaw.

I was just feeling sketchy, not invincible. Now I was consumed with a bitter taste in my mouth which had nothing to do with the drugs I had just ingested.

Thinking about Kristy always left a sour taste in my mouth though, that was no surprise. No matter how much time had passed or how many miles were between us, I was filled with an insurmountable anger which wouldn't quit.

Really, I had absolutely nothing to complain about. My life was what I had always wanted, at least on paper.

I was a millionaire, many times over with a fanbase and security. Women threw themselves at me in every country of the world and my songs were being heard all over the planet.

People screamed my name. Well, they screamed my stage name, Judas Crowe but it was still me whom they loved.

I had it all.

So why did the emptiness seem to smack me in the face like a sucker punch at the most bizarre times?

Like when I'm about to get a blowjob?

Kristy had damaged me more than I ever imagined she could.

I had never been able to tell Geneva the truth about why I'd taken the contract so quickly and without consulting her. The opportunity to provide for my baby had knocked and I had seized it, knowing that I would never again get a chance like that. What choice had I had?

How the fuck was I supposed to know that Kristy was a lying bitch and that she'd never been pregnant?

But by the time I'd learned the truth, Geneva was gone and no one would tell me where she was. I could have killed everyone at that point but my career swept me away from the recording studio to the world tour and by the time the smoke cleared, two years had passed.

I knew that Elsa had to know where Gen had gone but Jake wasn't taking my calls anymore and the idea of going back to Oakdale to confront everyone face-to-face was more than I could stomach.

I was worried what would happen if I saw Kristy, what I would do or say to her.

So I stayed away. And moved on with my life as if Jude LaCroix never really existed, even though I thought of Gen all the time, especially when we were recording.

I wondered if she heard our songs on the radio and thought of me. I don't know if I hoped she did or that she didn't.

Wherever she was, I hoped she was happy. I knew I owed my success to her. If it weren't for her pushing me, I would never have been signed.

Someone was pounding on the door to the suite and I turned back toward the room, debating whether to answer the door.

It was probably the groupie again, looking for another line.

I decided not to answer it but I began to clean up evidence of our all-night party, lest it was housekeeping.

"Jude?"

Ah shit. It was Hal.

I stood stalk still, hoping he would go away but the knocking persisted.

"Jude, I just saw the twinkie leave. I know you're in there!" my agent called in a singsong voice.

Double shit.

I sauntered toward the door, propping it open a crack.

"Hey," I said unenthusiastically. "You're back."

"I am and you look like hell," he greeted me, pushing his way inside the suite. His grey eyes instantly fell on the coffee table and his mouth twisted into a sardonic smirk.

"Again?" he growled, striding toward the silver tray. In one move, he scooped it up and disappeared. I could hear the water running in the kitchen as the rest of the eight ball was swept down the drain.

I didn't care – not really. I could buy more any time the mood struck which seemed to be with more and more frequency lately.

"You're on a slippery slope," Hal told me grimly. "You think this is all fun and games but the next thing you know, you're lying in rehab –"

"Okay! Okay!" I snapped. "Did you come here to lecture me or just say hi?"

"Neither," he retorted. "I came to get you idiots dressed. You and Trevor in particular."

"Dressed for what? We had the day before we leave," I groaned but I didn't know why I was arguing. The schedule was made to be upset, especially when there was downtime.

"There's a party tonight. Drake is hosting and you jackasses ended up on the guest list when he heard you were in town."

"Why don't we just move the party here?" I leered, motioning around the three-storey suite. "I think we have enough room."

"Just get your asses in gear. When music royalty

snaps, you jump. The limo will be downstairs at 8."

I blinked and glanced at my Rolex.

It was five thirty.

"You came here three hours early to tell me to get ready?" I laughed. "I'm not a chick."

"You're worse than a fucking chick," Hal snarled. "Go have a sauna and a shower. Get that shit out of your system and don't touch any more if you have it kicking around in here. I'm serious, Jude. Between you and that goddamned drummer, I'm at my wits' end with you."

"I'm not as bad as Trevor," I muttered, casting my eyes downward.

Hal scoffed.

"Once upon a time, Trevor said that about another bandmate. Guess where Louis is now?"

I didn't have to guess.

"When we're finished the tour at the end of the month, Trev is going to Aton in San Diego to dry out," Hal warned me. "Don't make me make a double reservation."

I didn't reply as Hal turned to leave.

"I know you think you're infallible," he added, staring at me with cold eyes. "But even the public had its limits, Jude. Manwhoring and coking are frowned upon now. This isn't the nineties."

He was gone before I could even come up with a snappy reply but he had given me some food for thought.

Besides the money and fame, had I really changed all that much since Oakland? I liked to think I had but staring around the shambles of my hotel suite, I wondered if that was true.

I reached for a half-drunk beer on the coffee table and took a sip, grimacing as the warm liquid touched my lips.

Oddly, a picture of Geneva popped into my mind, clearly, as if she was standing in front of me, shaking her head.

I'd been thinking of her more than usual the past few days and that would explain why I had been amplifying the self-abuse.

It made sense that she'd been on my mind, the stress of the life getting to me, just as it had gotten to her but more than that, I felt like she was close, calling out to me in some weird way.

Of course, that was nonsense. I had no doubt in my mind that if Gen ever thought of me, her memories were filled with venom and fury, not the sweet nothings I'd whispered into her ears as we lay entangled in one another, night after night.

Whatever the reason, I could almost hear her voice as she stared at me in my mind's eye.

"Are you happy now?" she asked and I snickered.

"Is that a philosophical question?"

"It's a real question," she replied. "Are you happy?"

"No," I said, surprising myself. "No, I'm not."

"Why not?"

"I'm missing something."

"Like what?"

I lifted my head and stared at her, my heart growing heavy as I shook my head.

"I don't know," I answered truthfully. "Maybe I'll never be happy."

She smiled but it was sad.

"Maybe not," she agreed.

Gen disappeared as she always did, leaving me standing alone, surrounded by luxury and nothingness. I silently willed her to return, to give me some meaning to whatever it was I was seeking but of course, she didn't. She was a figment of my imagination and my mind didn't want to accept that at the core, I was lonely even in the midst of a million people.

I was homesick for a small town and my weirdo roommate who had professed his love for my girlfriend.

Some days, I even longed for the sanctuary of the graveyard and my riding mower.

But most of all, I missed the sense of togetherness I'd had with Geneva, something I'd been chasing like a junky chases his first high.

Whatever had happened between Gen and I was gone and I knew that but it didn't keep the dull ache inside me from weaning.

No number of drugs or alcohol would smother that feeling and I had to accept that I was destined to be alone with my millions and Grammys.

I sighed heavily, realizing that the sun was already setting as I had sat wrapped in my reverie.

The time for self-pity was over. I had another vapid party to prepare for.

13

JUDE

I was drunk by the time we congregated to meet the limo in the lobby and I had nearly bowed out of the party in favor of sleep but I had a feeling that my agent would have come in to cup me by the ear and drag me out of the suite if I did.

"This is such bullshit," Corey muttered, his face pressed to his phone. "He promised us a night off."

I eyed the bassist skeptically, knowing that he was texting his wife as we piled into the stretch car.

If anyone should want to go out and party, I would have thought it would be Corey. When else did he get an escape? If he wasn't on the road, he was home with the old ball and chain.

And yet, Corey seemed to relish every second he had with his wife.

I was like that with Geneva before I couldn't figure my own shit out, I recalled and I realized that I was jealous of my band mate's relationship with his wife.

I admit, I couldn't envision myself married but I did remember how it felt to want to be with someone all the time.

I thought of the day I'd sat in the trailer park for hours, hoping to just get a glimpse of her.

"We're in and out," I vowed but Trevor whooped.

"Are you kidding?" he demanded. "Canadian chicks are easy! You're not dragging me out of a party at Drake's cottage for another platinum."

I stifled a groan and we all fell into silence, turning to watch the bright lights of Toronto begin to fade away.

"Where are we going?" I asked the driver after we'd been driving for forty-five minutes. "We've gotta be out of the city by now."

"Muskoka," the driver replied through the lowered partition but the answer meant nothing to me.

"It's cottage country, outside of the city," Corey volunteered. "It's nice but it takes a while to get there."

I groaned loudly and set the partition back up. Not only had I been suckered into this damned event, it was practically in another country.

Why did I have the feeling the night was only going to get worse from there?

∽

I HAD TO ADMIT, IT WAS STUNNING. THERE was nothing "cottage" about the sprawling estate house that sat atop a hill, encased in trees and spilled down to a private lake which was, incredibly, called Lake Rousseau.

Gen really was with me that night and as I wandered through the firefly lit lawn, passing by a kidney-shaped pool and two hot tubs, I half-expected to see her in the face of every brunette in my path.

It was a who's who of music at the party, a mesh

of hip hop artists, rock stars and rappers, intertwined with some actors and producers. I recognized half a dozen basketball players and a couple members of the Blue Jays mingling about.

Five years ago, I would have been on the floor, gasping for breath in my excitement at seeing all these famous people. Today, I just wanted to find a quiet spot by the lake and skip stones away from everyone.

When had I become so desensitized to it all?

"Jude?"

I turned at the sound of my name before I could stop myself.

"Hey Ash," I replied, offering the familiar face a quick smile. She wasn't the worst person I could have run into."

"I haven't seen you in a while," I told her.

"Unlucky for me," she purred, putting her hand on my arm suggestively. I grinned and shrugged it off.

"How's everything going in your scene?"

"Oh, you know me. I can always use a little more rock and a little less country," she replied. The innuendo wasn't designed to be subtle and it wasn't. At all.

In some circles, Ashleigh Chambers was God. If you got in with her, your dreams would be granted, particularly if you were young and attractive.

Thankfully for me, I didn't need her but that didn't stop the overripe cougar from trying to sink her claws into me at every opportunity.

"I'm surprised to see you here," I confessed. "Canada? Doesn't seem like your demographic. At least not Toronto."

"Oh," she chuckled. "I'm showcasing my latest talent. Actually, you're from Louisiana too, aren't you, sugar?"

"I am," I replied. "What's his name?"

"Her. Juniper Jane."

I blinked, trying to remember where I'd heard that name before.

"Why do I know that name?" I asked, my brow furrowing. "Has she been on the radio?"

"She just debuted – oh, there she is. June! June, over here honey!"

She waved frantically and I turned my head.

When I saw her, I felt like time stopped and it all unfolded.

Fuck! Of course. Juniper Jane. How could I have forgotten?

She hadn't seen me yet and I inhaled sharply, the wind knocked completely from my lungs as Gen approached me, her short, blonde bob barely moving as she approached.

"Juniper, this is Judas Crowe," Ashleigh announced as Gen neared and I saw her freeze in her tracks as she stared at me. A look of sheer disbelief crossed her face as her dark eyes rested on mine.

"He's the lead singer of No Excuse."

Ashleigh beamed at her but there was no smile on Geneva's face.

"Hey Gen," I said, unsure of how to react. Could I give her a hug? God, I wanted to touch her, to kiss her lips, to find out what she'd been doing for the last four years.

Oh God, she was beautiful. As beautiful as she'd always been. Although the brassy blonde obviously made her uncomfortable, she was still driving me crazy.

Why had she done it when she had been so steadfast against selling out?

What had changed her mind? After so long? Did it have anything to do with me?

"Juniper, you can say hello," Ashleigh chided her as if she was a child and I watched as a completely stoic expression crossed over her face.

"Hello Mr. Crowe," she said. "Excuse me."

She spun and wandered away, leaving me staring after her in shock. Ashleigh scowled at her.

"Don't mind Juniper," she grimaced. "She still thinks she's living in the bayou."

"She's not from the bayou," I replied automatically and Ashleigh's eyebrows shot up.

"You know her?" she asked, her eyes widening with interest but I was watching as Gen disappeared into the crowd.

"We knew each other...once."

Ashleigh squealed, clapping her hands together in excitement.

"That is fantastic!" she gasped. "Oh, then you know she sings like an angel."

"She does," I confirmed. "Her voice gives me goose pimples."

"I wonder what the two of you would sound like together."

I barely heard what she was suggesting as I lost sight of Geneva in the throng of people.

"Excuse me, Ashleigh. I'll catch up with you later."

I didn't hear her response and I bolted off toward where I'd seen her vanish. I had been right; Gen had been near enough to touch all this time.

But it was obvious she didn't want to see me and I knew I shouldn't be pursuing her. Still, I couldn't stop myself. I needed to know how she was doing at the very least.

It didn't take me long to catch up with her, the

red of her halter top catching my attention as I entered the three-storey cottage but she was retreating up the stairs.

"Jude! Hey Jude!" A chorus of people called after me but I ignored them, my sights strictly on Geneva as she stole through the second floor and entered a room at the end of the hall.

"Gen open the door," I called, knocking on it quickly. "I just want to talk to you for a second."

"Sorry, this bathroom is occupied," came the flat response.

"Geneva, please. Just talk to me for a minute."

Silence met my plea and I stood in the hallway like an idiot, debating what to do. I couldn't keep knocking on the door like some stalker but I knew I couldn't walk away without seeing her again, even for a minute.

"Gen, please. Just give me five minutes and I swear, I'll never bother you again."

A few seconds later, the lock clicked and the door opened slightly. I gently shoved it open.

Gen was sitting on the counter, staring straight ahead at the far wall as if I wasn't there.

"Holy shit," I breathed. "I can't believe it's you!"

"Yep, it's me."

Her words were clipped and she refused to meet my eyes, even as I put myself directly in front of her. It was like she was staring right through me.

"I can see you're still pissed at me but Gen, I did look for you. Jake wouldn't tell me where you went and – "

"It's fine. That's ancient history, Jude."

There was so little emotion in her words, my heart froze slightly.

"Will you please look at me?"

She didn't.

"Gen, I owe you an explanation. You need to know why I left so suddenly and without you."

"No, I don't!"

Finally, there was something in her voice and maybe it wasn't what I wanted to hear but it was a hell of a lot better than nothing at all.

"Kristy, the girl who was with me, came to me and told me she was pregnant."

It was the first time I had disclosed that information to anyone and the statement hung in the air like stale cigarette smoke, putrid and choking.

"What?" she choked. "Kristy had your baby?"

I shook my head.

"No," I sighed. "No, she was threatened by you and made it up to get me back. She was never pregnant but I didn't find out until well after I'd left for LA."

Her chocolate eyes narrowed and a cruel smile formed on her face.

"So you just ran when you heard she was pregnant."

"What? No!" I shook my head, cocking my head to stare at her in disbelief. "I took the deal because they were offering me a shit ton of money on the spot, Gen. I didn't have a pot to piss in if you recall, and I couldn't imagine how I was going to provide for my kid when I couldn't even afford my own place. I didn't run – just the opposite."

She studied my face with parted lips and I could see the wheels turning in her mind.

"You stayed in contact with Kristy after you left?"

"I sent that bitch half of my signing bonus which she never gave back," I snorted. "And she sent me fake ultrasounds and baby name ideas."

Geneva's olive tone seemed to pale significantly.

"I wanted to tell you right away but you were so angry at me that night when you told me to leave. I texted you and called you. And then you were gone."

"Oh my God..."

"I don't expect you to forgive me for the way we left things, Gen but I don't want there to be any bad blood between us. Who knows? We could end up working together again."

She gaped at me and I lost my tentative smile.

"You've been cashing in on songs we wrote together," she choked. "How am I supposed to overlook that?"

My eyes bulged.

"No!" I insisted. "Your name is on the songs. All the songs. You can check the trademarks!"

"What?"

"You're getting royalties for the songs, Gen. Hasn't anyone contacted you?"

"No..."

Her voice was barely a whisper and I no longer understood the expression on her face. Was she still angry or sad? Maybe confused? I had given her a lot to absorb for one sitting.

"Gen, say something please? Or slap my face or something."

She swallowed visibly, raising her head to meet my eyes and suddenly I recognized what she was feeling as I'd seen it hundreds of times before.

"I missed you," she breathed, tears filling her dark eyes and I stepped closer to her, as her palms touched my face. "God, I really missed you."

"God, I missed you too," I murmured and as I said it, I knew that I had never spoken truer words.

"Kiss me," she urged, yanking my face toward her and I didn't need to be told twice because for the first time in years, I felt that cloud of gloom lift off my head, disappearing fully as our lips meshed together.

Maybe I did know what I'd needed to be happy all along.

14
GENEVA

What are you doing? What are you doing? What are you doing?

Over and over the voice screamed at me but I wouldn't stop what I had started. For years I had lived in a perpetual state of tension, walking around, afraid to let anyone in as I hid my children from their father.

I had been so convinced that Jude had run away, leaving me and all his responsibilities behind without so much as a second thought but I had been wrong, so wrong.

The opposite had occurred in fact.

He had tried to step up, to be a man and do the right thing. He had risked our relationship to do right by his unborn child, a fake child who never existed.

All along, he could have been the father Cheyenne and Wyatt needed but I had kept them from him in my own bitterness.

I kissed him harder as if to suppress my guilt, to alleviate the shame I was feeling. When he found out about what I'd done, he would never forgive me and I could not blame him.

His hot mouth trailed along the curve of my throat, his lips suctioning to my skin as his tongue jutted out to lick the saltiness of my skin.

My naked calves wrapped around his waist, drawing him closer to me on the countertop, needing to feel his bulge against the heat of my middle. How many times had I fantasized about being with him again, even in the depth of my anger? He was exactly where I'd always wanted him and I wanted to relish every second we had because I knew this could be our last.

Not could be. Will be.

My halter top slipped over my head, my breasts exposed fully and he pushed me back against the counter, his mouth locking onto the taut skin of my nipple as his fingers tweaked and teased the other.

It was like we'd never been apart, our crevices melding together like they were designed to fit and I mewled when his teeth gnashed at me gently, sending shivers through my body.

He pulled me closer to the edge of the counter and I fell back on my elbows, watching him as his mouth moved across my belly button, down between my thighs.

"I've dreamt about tasting you one more time," he growled, peeling my soaked panties aside, nuzzling into my scorched center. The vibrations on my clit sent shots of pleasure up and down my spine and when he raised my knees over his shoulders, I was ready for his long laps.

He licked at me vigorously and I was so tense, my nerves would have twanged if he'd plucked them but I was lost in the sensation of his reverberating mouth, kissing my swollen lips.

I was going to cum and I cried out, my fingers curling almost backward as I clung to the marble of the countertop.

"Oh fuck," he muttered. "You're squirting."

I'd never done that before but I covered his face with my juices in a mist, my climax seemingly endless.

I was so caught up in my release, I barely noticed that he'd risen, spreading my thighs apart as his massive shaft slid across my cleft, his eyes boring into me.

"You belong with me," he told me, plunging himself inside me as I stared at him with glassy eyes.

I had forgotten how big he was, how well he filled me, even though I hadn't been with another man since our time together. It seemed impossible that anyone could feel so good and I squeezed myself about him, locking my ankles at his back and urging him in further.

Slow and deep he thrust into me, our gazes never faltering.

"Say it," he ordered me, his words short and gasping. "Say you belong with me."

"I..." I couldn't handle it, the depth of him, the way he stared at me, the sound of his voice. He had the same effect on me as he always had and I couldn't stop the second orgasm from mounting.

"I – I'm cumming," I screeched. He pounded me then, falling forward to pin me mercilessly to the surface and I screamed until my voice was raw, my nail drawing blood on his back this time when they caught his skin.

"Good," he breathed, his own frame rigid and I felt his sack tighten against my ass. "Good."

He spilled into me in deep, hot spurts, each stroke thicker than the last.

My thighs were quivering violently when he finally stopped but I continued to flex the walls of my pussy, drawing out every last drop of his seed.

He lay on top of me, trying to catch his breaths and I savored the feel of his moist skin to mine.

I couldn't resist pressing my mouth to the saline flesh, inhaling his scent as he withdrew from me. My heart was still pounding because I knew it was my opportunity to tell him everything but I wasn't sure if I was ready to do it.

He deserves to know. Cheyenne and Wyatt deserve their father and he's not who you thought he was.

"Are you okay?" he asked when he saw I wasn't moving.

"Yeah," I replied, sitting up. "That was...unexpected."

He grinned and shook his head and I looked at him closely for the first time, without emotions clouding me, without biases blurring my vision.

He was thinner than he had been and he looked exhausted.

I'd looked like that once and I'd look like that again when Ashleigh was finished with me. I wondered if Jude was regretting his choice but I didn't ask.

Even if he was, he wouldn't tell me.

"You sold out," he said and my back jammed upward like there was a rod stuck in it.

"What?"

"You're Juniper June. I thought that was why you got out when you did."

I pursed my lips together.

"Circumstances changed," I replied. "Suddenly it didn't seem so bad."

He zipped up his pants and looked at me.

"Yeah? Then why do you look so unhappy?"

I blinked at the observation. Even after all that time, did he still know me or was that just a lucky guess?

My heart knew the answer; he'd always known me, even though we'd only been together a short time.

We'd written together, slept together, performed together and now we had children together. He knew me better than anyone knew me.

"I don't much care for being a blonde. Or the name Juniper," I replied lightly, leaning back against the counter to stare at him.

"I'll have to agree with you on both points," he laughed.

Stepping toward me, he gathered me in his arms and kissed the top of my head.

"I'm sorry we've lost so much time but we can make it up, Gen. I've been so lost without you these past years and I don't know what you've been up to but – "

"No."

I blurted it out before I had a chance to stop myself.

"No?" he echoed in confusion. "No what?"

"No, this was good. Thank you."

I turned to leave, wondering what the hell was wrong with me but I quickly realized that I couldn't spring the news about his secret twins on him inside a bathroom.

Why not? That's how I learned about them, I reasoned.

"Thank you?" he repeated. "Seriously? You're going to do this again?"

I turned to look at him, a bemused expression on his face but I could sense an underlying anger there too.

"I'm at a weird place in my life right now, Jude and – "

"You're always at a fucking weird place, Gen. You're never settled, you're never sure. You call me impulsive but you're indecisive as fuck."

My mouth parted slightly at the accusation but I suddenly saw that he was right.

Everything I'd ever done in my life was wishy-washy. I couldn't decide. I couldn't see anything through.

Except the twins. That was the only thing I'd committed to and stuck through from beginning to end.

"Don't walk out of here without some guarantee that I'm going to hear from you, Gen, please?"

He was pleading with me to do the right thing and I was on the fence. What was wrong with me? How could this even be a question?

"Do you want to get out of here?" I asked suddenly and his face exploded in relief.

"Yeah," he said. "I really do."

I nodded.

"Me too."

∽

I'D BEEN TO DRAKE'S COTTAGE ONE TIME before and I remembered there was a fleet of random boats at the dock.

We found ourselves in a rowboat, under the moon and I peered up at the sky, a soft smile on my face.

"Do you miss the star living in LA?" I asked.

"You know I'm living in LA?"

I was embarrassed at being caught.

"I've heard bits and pieces about you," I answered softly, glad that despite the bright stars, my face was still hidden in the shadows.

We paddled far enough out that the party was barely noticeable and stopped to drift.

"Where did you go?"

"I was staying with my brother in Lafayette until two weeks ago. Now we're in Nashville."

"We're? Your brother moved there too?"

Shit. Shit. Shit.

"No. Not my brother."

"Then who are *we*? You did say we, didn't you?" he pressed.

I didn't reply, thinking of how I was going to tell him what I wanted to say.

"Yes."

It wasn't necessary to look at his face. The disappointment emanating from him was palpable.

"You're married," he sighed, reaching for a paddle. "I'm sorry. I didn't know or I certainly wouldn't have pursued you, Gen. I hope you know that."

"I'm not married."

"And I'm not arguing semantics with you," he snapped. "Married or boyfriend who is expecting you home, it's all the same to me."

"I don't have a boyfriend expecting me home. I have two kids."

He dropped the paddle and it almost slipped into the lake but I dipped forward to catch it.

"Oh...wow..." he blubbered. "Uh, congratulations. How old? Boys or girls?"

He was doing rote questioning, digging into his list of platitude inquiries when delivered baby news.

"They are three. Twins."

I waited for him to do the math but he still seemed stunned by the revelation.

"Wow," he said again, apparently grasping for something else to say. "Wow."

I continued to stare at him but his mind wasn't going there, not yet.

"Jude," I sighed, sick of waiting for him.

"Hm?"

"They're yours."

"What?"

"The twins. They're yours. Their names are Cheyenne and Wyatt. They look exactly like you."

The shock on his face was unlike anything I'd ever seen, not even in the movies. His jaw had dropped so far that I was surprised it didn't touch the bottom of the boat.

"Is this a joke?" he asked. "Some sick way of getting back at me for not telling you about Kristy?"

I shook my head miserably. This was going worse than I had initially envisioned.

"No," I whispered. "There are twins and they are yours."

I reached into my purse to pull out my phone, showing him the home screen where my children grinned toothily at the camera.

He was paler than the moonlight as he studied their small features, his fingers trailing over the case in awe.

Suddenly, he turned and hauled the phone into the lake.

"You're a twisted bitch, Gen. This is wrong, no matter how mad you are. If you're looking for a payout, you're barking up the wrong tree."

I gaped at him, certain I'd misunderstood him.

"You think that what? I tracked you to Canada to a party in order to blackmail you into a shitty payout?" I laughed but there was no mirth in my voice. I was madder than hell. In my wildest imagination, I never would have thought he would think I was that pathetic.

"I don't know what your game is," he snarled, grabbing for the oars and starting back to the pier. "But I don't want any part of it."

"You don't want any part of your children?"

"They aren't my children!" He howled, his voice carrying across the lake and suddenly I realized he was still in shock.

I reached forward and grabbed his forearm.

"They are."

His eyes shifted to me and he stared at me blankly.

"They are," I said again. "Wyatt and Cheyenne. They are your twins."

A long, devastating silence ensued and all the fire abruptly faded from his eyes.

"You kept my children from me for three years?"

I felt like I'd been stabbed and I swallowed the boulder in my throat.

"I'm sorry," I whispered. "I'm so sorry, Jude."

He jerked his arm back and continued to row, his jaw locking with determination.

"Yeah," he spat. "So am I."

15

JUDE

Trevor smashed the drum, cuing my entrance and I flew onto the stage, twanging my guitar as I moved.

I had earplugs but they did nothing to alleviate the din of the crowd who screamed until their faces were crimson, waving wildly to capture my attention.

"I made a mistake, it's been all I can take but you're gone again…"

The cheering was defeating but I kept on with the song, trying not to feel the burn of tears threatening me as I sang.

Every time No Excuse performed this song, I could see Gen smiling at me in the Fontaine, staring into my eyes as she waited for her part.

"You begged me to go, but now I know that you wanted me near and we're bound till the end."

This was the first time I'd sung it since her soul-crushing confession in Toronto.

"And I'm leaving...leaving this time...leaving this time to stay," I crooned. "And you can't...you can't...you can't keep me away."

It was taking every fiber of my being not to turn and run for the wings, yet another place which always reminded me of the girl, of the first night we'd performed at JoJo's together to a packed house.

I wanted to find her, to find my kids and bury my head in their heads, inhaling the smell of them. I wanted to bolt from that sold-out show and hop on the first plane to Nashville, say screw my contract and screw the band and screw everything.

But of course, I couldn't.

I had commitments and I wouldn't be able to meet my kids for another three weeks. What would I do then? What would I say to Gen?

I knew I had to shove them all from my mind, to forget about them until I was at least alone.

Performing in front of fifteen thousand people was not the place to lose control, no matter how on the edge I was.

Even as I thought it, I realized I'd missed a cue but my adoring fans didn't seem to care.

Hal will care.

Now was not the time to throw everything away.

Once again, I had to put Geneva on the back burner. And with her, my children.

~

"I'm not sticking around," I told Trevor. "I'm tired."

"Yeah, you sang like ass tonight," the drummer agreed. "Lay off the sauce the night before. You sound like you've been crying."

I chewed on the insides of my cheeks and fought my way through the crowds with my security detail, pausing to sign some autographs on the way out but my heart wasn't in it, not anymore.

My heart wasn't in anything.

"Your car is out back, Mr. Crowe," Hank told me, maneuvering me out of the busy amphitheater.

I followed him out through the alleyway and to my relief, I saw that there was only a small crowd gathered there. It wasn't as bad as some of the places I'd been.

"Step aside, please," my linebacker detail intoned, his arms out.

"Is that him, mama?"

My head jerked at the sound of such a small voice in an alleyway at that hour of the night. It was after eleven o'clock.

"Ma'am, please step aside."

Suddenly she appeared, ducking under Hank's extended arms.

"Are you Jude?"

I was taken aback by the toddler's face staring up defiantly at me but my heart stopped as I instantly recognized her.

"Lady, is this your kid?" Hank yelled.

"It's okay," I choked, dropping to my knees. "Are you Cheyenne?"

She cocked her head to the side and studied me with skepticism.

"Maybe. But I asked you first."

"I'm Jude," I told her, extending my hand. Suddenly, another tiny face appeared, a boy who was undoubtedly her twin.

"Lady, come and get your damned kids!" Hank howled and I glanced up to see Gen standing off to the side, watching the twins interact with me.

"Hank, it's all right," I called to him. "Put her and the kids in the limo. They're coming with me."

The security guard looked surprised by the request but it wasn't his way to ask questions and he instantly obliged as I rose and offered the kids my hands.

"Can I hold yours?"

"Sure!" they chorused.

"Mama says you're a friend," Cheyenne added. "We don't hold hands with strangers."

"Your mama is a smart woman," I choked as the door opened and we slid inside, Gen close behind. She still had not said a word but I could see she was fighting to show her true feelings on her face.

"We like you," Wyatt volunteered and I couldn't tear my eyes from their faces. God, they looked so much like me. I would be a fool to deny they were mine when anyone could see plain as day who they belonged to.

"Yeah. Mama says we could stay up to meet you tonight so we like you," Cheyenne agreed and I could already see that she was the assertive one of the pair.

"I hope you like me for more than that later on," I sighed, finally managing to tear my eyes away from them to look at their mother.

"Mama says you're a rock star," Cheyenne offered. "I like rocks."

I laughed and blinked quickly, knowing I was about to cry.

"Where to, Mr. Crowe?" the driver asked.

I looked at Geneva and shrugged.

"Where are you staying?" I asked.

"At your place."

"Back to the hotel, Pierre," I told him.

We stared at each other for a long moment and I shook my head.

"I don't understand," I mumbled. "What are you even doing in Paris?"

"We followed you," Gen replied quietly. "I thought about how unfair what I did to you was and I realized that you had to wait until you got home to meet the twins. So I brought the twins to you."

I squinted as I looked at her.

"Juniper is allowed to be a brunette again?" I asked curiously, noting her new hairstyle.

"No. Juniper said screw it again," she replied. "Geneva Rousseau is a brunette and it's not much but her YouTube channel has enough followers to bring in something for now. Who knows? Maybe down the line, I'll find someone who thinks that boring brunettes can make and sell music too."

"There is nothing boring about you," I reminded her, scooching in closer toward her but I stopped, remembering that I had two pairs of little green eyes following me.

"I'm proud of you, Gen," I told her huskily, watching at the twins sleepily explored the inside of the limo. I could see they were getting ready to crash. "You're amazing and I'm sorry about what I said about you being indecisive. You decided to be a mom and you are amazing. I don't know how you did it for so long and I wish I'd known sooner."

"You know now," she replied, tilting my head toward hers. "And together, I think we can raise two amazing human beings."

"Together?" I asked her sincerely. "Are we going to do this together?"

"Only if you want to," she replied quickly, dropping her hand from my face. "I didn't mean to be presumptuous. I just..."

"What?"

"I want us to be a family," she said in a rush. "I want us to be together but not if we're constantly wary of one another."

I nodded, realizing how much just saying that was a major step for her. She had matured. Motherhood had matured her and she had matured me.

We both had a lot of growing up to do but we'd managed – together.

"A tour will be rough on them," I murmured, pulling her into a hug. "They're so small."

"I know," she laughed. "I wasn't really going to fly them around the world but I wanted to make some grand gesture so that you know I'm serious about this, about having you in their lives. And I want you to know how sorry I am about everything that's happened."

"That makes two of us," I assured her, kissing the top of her head. "I'm glad you're here."

"Me too."

"You're kissing! Ew!" Cheyenne screeched and I guiltily dropped my arm from around Gen. She howled with laughter and embraced me.

"You better get used to seeing your mama and daddy hugging and kissing," she told them. "You're gonna see it a lot."

The twins peered up at us with sleepy eyes and I could see they didn't understand what was going on but that would take time.

"Would you like to come and snuggle?" Gen

suggested, extending her arms out to the children.

Instantly, they scrambled onto our laps and I was filled with such a sense of peace, I almost sobbed.

Was this what I had wanted all along? A family? Children?

Nothing had ever felt as right to me as life did at that moment.

"I love you," Geneva murmured, laying her head on my shoulder as our fingers swept through the blonde curls of the twins.

"I love you too," the three of us breathed back.

EPILOGUE

Geneva

"You look terrified," Jude whispered. "Take a deep breath."

I shook my head and peered out onto the stage, inhaling sharply as he drew me into his arms, smiling that now-familiar grin at me. It should have steadied my nerves but if anything it made me more anxious.

"You do it," I breathed. "I -I can't."

"What do you mean?" Jude demanded, peering down at my face in shock. "This is what we've been working toward for two years! Of course you can – and you will!"

I lowered my head mournfully, a thousand

doubts flooding through me. They weren't out there for me, they were out there for Jude. I wasn't Juniper Jane anymore, I had no following of my own. Jude had gained notoriety in his own right, branching out from No Excuse to go solo while we raised the twins.

I had been grateful to step out of the spotlight for a time, the taste of my sell-out personality still leaving an acrid taste in my mouth.

When had I ever made a decision and stuck to it? What was I doing there?

"You're second-guessing yourself again," Jude murmured as the din from the club outside swelled. "You're overthinking."

My mouth parted to argue but he knew me too well. He could read my distress all over my face.

"You go out first," I insisted. "Warm them up at least."

"No."

The word was flat and firm.

"Please, Jude? I – I think I made a mistake thinking I could do this. I'm a mom now, soccer parent and – "

"And you're a sister, a friend, my soulmate and my muse," he murmured, his emerald eyes boring into mine, dispelling all my fears as we shut the world out. "If it wasn't for you, no one would even know my name, Gen."

I felt myself relaxing, losing myself in the warmth of his hypnotic tones. He always knew just what to say, what to do to alleviate my crazy when it crept in on me.

I liked to think I did the same for him.

"You need to focus on me, just like we rehearsed," he told me, his words even, as if he was singing them to me. "We aren't here, we're in the trailer, pouring over sheet music. We're wrapped up in each other with the guitar. Close your eyes and picture it."

Inhaling shakily, I did what he suggested and the noise from beyond the stage faded away.

Suddenly, I was in the trailer but not recently. I was there in those early days, before the twins, before the heartbreak. We were laughing and struggling to find the right lyrics, making up silly words that didn't fit. There was a box of cold pizza and the scent of our lovemaking lingering around us.

In my mind's eye, the scene shifted and I saw Jude, lifting Cheyenne over his head, spinning her around like a helicopter as Wyatt squealed for his turn and then we were all staring at our new house in Baton Rogue, the four of us huddled beneath the loblolly pines, the scent of gardenias wafting up from the garden to meet my nose.

Slowly, I opened my eyes and smiled at him, realizing that what he said was true. So much had changed since we had first met. My priorities were different now but my heart was still very much the same. There was room enough for my love of family and my love of music.

Jude had given me everything I ever wanted, proven here as the crowd outside waited for us to make our debut.

"There she is," he chuckled, noting the relief in my eyes. "Crisis averted?"

"Yes," I breathed. "I'm ready."

He nodded, clasping my hand and tugging me through the wings.

As the curtain cleared my face, we met with the band onstage and a roar of approval greeted us. Instantly, my eyes fell on familiar faces at the front of the packed club and my pulse quickened again to make me lightheaded.

"What are they doing here?" I cried as Jude led me to the mics. He grinned boyishly and waved at Elsa and the others who seemed bursting with pride sandwiched between a mass of adoring fans.

"They're here for you, obviously," he whispered back and I was speechless with gratitude. They were all there, Jake, Marybeth and her husband, Charlie, Carrie and her boyfriend. I hadn't called them. I didn't want them to see if I failed on our first night before a live audience. This wasn't YouTube. This wasn't a series of "likes" and trolls. This was the real deal. We would know if we had what it took as a couple, if I had what it took at Geneva Rousseau, not Juniper Jane.

But I was so glad they had taken the trip to LA, knowing that finding sitters and taking time off work couldn't be easy for them. I couldn't believe that Jude had called them, knowing they still had not forgiven him, even after all that time.

"Ladies and gents," Jude called. "Thank you all for coming to our debut live show."

Hoots and cheers followed his announcement but Jude held up his hand, peering at me through his peripheral vision.

"Some of you know me," he continued as the din settled slightly. "Most of you know my beautiful girlfriend and mother of my children, Geneva."

My heart almost exploded with outpouring of screams which ensued and I blinked quickly, overcome by emotion as I saw that they really were there for both of us.

"We've been through a lot together," Jude continued, his voice carrying somehow, despite our fans' vocal adoration. "A lot of crazy shit, in fact, most of it mine."

Appreciative laughter.

"So," Jude said, turning toward me, his eyes gleaming with love. "I wrote this for Geneva because, without her, I'd be nothing but a wasted soul, strumming through life without purpose."

He reached for his guitar and strapped it over his shoulder, playing lightly as the bassist found his line.

This wasn't part of the show and I stood, watching him curiously.

"What are you doing?" I mouthed, my brow furrowing in confusion but he was focussed on the song which I had never heard.

"You held me together even when I was gone," he sang, a sweet, melancholic tune flowing through me. "You gave me the strength to carry on."

A lump formed in my throat as a few light whoops escaped the patrons.

"I never knew was missing in my life..."

Our eyes met and I couldn't stop a single tear from sliding down my cheek when he dropped to his knee and beamed up at me, a gasp emanating from my lips.

"But I know now that I need you for my wife..."

I didn't hear anything else as I knocked him to the stage, smothering his face with kisses, the shock of the moment overwhelming me. I didn't need to hear anything else.

Jude laughed as I straddled him, his father's guitar still pressed between us as I finally lifted my head to stare at him. There was no one else there even though I could hear the insanity from somewhere above me.

"Is that a yes?" he asked and I laughed, full streaks of tears streaming my face as I nodded.

"Of course it's a yes," I whispered, leaning forward to kiss his lips. "Are you sure this is what you want? I mean – "

"Am I sure that I want to grow old with you, the mother of my children, my inspiration and the best thing that ever happened to me? Yes, I'm sure."

"We've – we've just never talked about it," I murmured. "Why now?"

"Because, Gen, the thought of ever being without you makes me sick inside. I was away from you and our babies long enough and whatever ride we're about to embark upon, here, tonight, I want to do it unified."

"Would you say yes already and get the show started?" Marybeth yelled onto the stage, breaking the bubble around us.

I turned to glare at her playfully.

"I already did!" I called back.

"Whoo hoo!"

"Come on," I laughed, reluctantly climbing off him. "We better start the show before they start throwing tomatoes."

We stood but I couldn't resist sneaking in one last kiss before claiming my mic. Our time had come finally and no matter what happened that night or any other, we wouldn't be apart again.

"Let's do this!" Jude cried and the drummer kicked off our first song together with a smash of the cymbals.

Yes, I thought happily. *Let's do this thing called life. Together.*

- The End -

LETTER TO THE READERS

Dear reader, thank you so much for taking the chance to read my book. I hope you've enjoyed reading Jude and Geneva's story as much as I've enjoyed writing it.

This is just the start of the entire Baby Fever series, and I can't wait for you to find out what I've got for you in the stories that follow! (Spoiler alert: there will be an accidental marriage, a bad boy next door, billionaire twins and even a sexy mountain man! ;))

Seriously, I love how dramatic these two are. They both are clearly very emotional and have a hard time expressing their feelings. At first, they couldn't handle their own emotions and that caused them a lot of troubles. Have you ever experienced that? And Geneva had to learn how to be a mother with her twins...I was just so glad that fate brought them back together again.

I've had zero experience dating musicians. Well, maybe, if I have to count, I met a piano teacher from Belgium during my trip to Europe in 2014. He was extremely emotional and romantic, and he even wanted to follow me back home at the end of my vacation, but I was too rational to let him do so. Now I still think of him from time to time. Maybe I even got my inspirations from him!

Anyway, I'd love to hear your love stories with musicians. I'm sure some of you are into the wild rock star types.

Please, if you enjoyed the story, help a girl out by leaving a short review for this book. It will only take a few seconds, and I'd really appreciate it!

Also, if you'd like to join me on another journey to Vegas, turn to the next page and read the first few chapters of book 2 in the series. This one is called *Accidental Soulmates*, and it's a Vegas accidental marriage romance. It'll be a fun and sultry read, I assure you. So turn to the next page to read it now!

Love,

Nicole

SNEAK PEEK: ACCIDENTAL SOULMATES

Baby Fever Book 2

PROLOGUE

The Dream

From somewhere behind him, a blast of raucous laughter caused him to start, distracting him from the blazing machines inside the casino.

Julian turned his head slightly to the side, toward the noise and eyed the overweight, bleached blonde who couldn't have been from anywhere other than Texas. The machine screeched and winnings poured out the lip in a waterfall of coins.

"Lookie, Patrick! I dun won four hundred

smackeroos!" she chortled in a voice which fit her obnoxious appearance perfectly. Naturally, it was wrought with a deep Texan drawl.

Patrick, who apparently stood at her side, nodded approvingly and grinned a toothless smile.

"Ya sure did, Colleen! I knew you'd make our rent this time!"

Even as he thought it, a voice echoed his sentiments perfectly.

"Charming," someone muttered from his left, her low, sultry tone laced with contempt. Julian's eyes traveled toward the woman at his side who watched the scene with a full mouth twisted in a fusion of disdain and something he couldn't quite decipher.

Wistfulness?

Longing?

It was difficult to read, especially since she had such a classically beautiful face, almost as if she had descended from royalty with high cheekbones and large, guarded eyes. It wasn't as if she was suspicious per se but shadowed by the woes of life. It was hard to say what she might see in the scene which made her sad—the fact that they had won or that they were a couple.

"You're not a fan of the machines?" he asked and she cast him a look of surprise. For a moment, Julian felt that he was invisible and she was staring directly through him with her golden-brown eyes.

Am I here? He asked himself and he idly wondered if he had spoken the question aloud. The ecstasy he had taken in his suite was causing his body to tingle in a peculiar way and if he looked at the girl a certain way, he saw her split in two.

I'd like to split her in two, he thought, a wide grin forming on his generous mouth, the abrasive woman at the slots all but forgotten.

Taking drugs was not really his scene but the impromptu vacation to Vegas had brought back some old college boy in him and he reasoned that without supervision, he was entitled to let loose once in a while.

"I really haven't had much experience in casinos," the raven-haired girl replied and Julian's eyes moved along the slender lines of her neck toward the swelling breasts threatening to spill out of her too-small t-shirt.

He wondered if she had done that by design or if she just desperately needed a new wardrobe.

Julian suddenly had the irresistible urge to take her shopping.

"Casinos are overrated," he told her, extending his hand toward her. "I know a much better way to see Vegas."

She eyed his extended hand and for a moment, Julian thought she was going to slap him. The heady feeling of the drug made him laugh at the image and he almost welcomed the feel of her palm on his cheek. He was feeling much more brazen, not to say he was ever shy. But at the same time, he felt as if he might shatter into a million pieces if she didn't accept his hand. In the end, she took it, raising her head back slightly to look up at him with an almost child-like wonder.

"Show me," she told him.

He didn't catch her name—or perhaps he never asked. It didn't seem important as the hours flew past, her throaty laughter bringing him higher. Every second he spent with her brought him closer to the need to possess her.

Julian found himself calling her "Kitten" because she reminded him so much as a sexy little beast but there was something inherently wicked about her, a mischievous undertone beneath those serious eyes which he was dying to unleash. He knew she would be a wildcat in bed...if they got that far.

Something primitive inside him told Julian they would.

He fulfilled his desire to take her shopping, insisting that the extravagant wardrobe be sent to his suite and the afternoon flittered into night, Julian losing himself inside her golden eyes.

"Are you real?" he asked her at one point and she cocked her head to the side, a long strand of hair dripping over the luscious curve of her breasts. It was a pressing question, one which echoed over and over in his mind like a chant. Julian licked his lips, the desire to taste the cream of her skin overwhelming him.

"Are you?" she replied, spinning to fan him in a strand of black tresses.

There were champagne and lobster at the Chart House and drinks at Caesar's. Slowly, his memory began to fade and all that remained was the haunting glow of her strange eyes which tantalized him lured him back to his rooms at the Palazzo.

When he finally gathered her in his arms, it was everything he had envisioned from the moment he had heard her voice.

"Kiss me," she ordered him. "Hard."

He didn't need to be told a second time and when their lips crushed together, it was as if she had cast a spell on him. The bulge in his pants poked dangerously through the material of his crotch. He could feel her heat through the worn material of her denim jeans.

She tasted sweet and liquored but when their tongues met and Julian's hands cupped the breasts which had been taunting him all night, the feeling that he was floating consumed him entirely and he was spun toward the ceiling, watching their clothes falling to the floor, among the packages he had purchased for her.

Why didn't she change into one of the dresses I bought her? He wondered irrelevantly but there was no time to consider her reasoning, not when her mouth moved along his ripped, naked pecs and toward the belt of his pants. She paused to tease his taut nipples with a lashing tongue.

Julian's palms reluctantly fell away from the full Cs and atop her silken crown of hair, sighing heavily as her hot breath touched the skin of his waistline. His organ was rigid, ready and waiting for her to take.

A warm, soft hand cupped his sack, moving his shaft into her mouth and down her throat with a fluid, easy motion. She was hot and wet, her mouth hoovering around him in a vortex of desire.

Julian groaned, closing his eyes, meaning to relish the sensation but suddenly, it was over.

When he opened his eyes, the black-haired vixen was gone and he lay sprawled against the still-made king bed of his hotel room.

He was fully dressed in a tuxedo he had not been wearing the previous night. Sitting up, he gazed about, blinking gritty eyes. The ecstasy had depleted the water supply to his body and he desperately needed hydration.

Did I dream that woman in a drug-induced haze? He asked himself, half-crawling, half-stumbling toward the bar. But when he arrived in the sunken living room, he saw the thousands of dollars in women's clothing sitting untouched in piles.

"Kitten?" he called out weakly but as he said the word, he felt foolish and clamped his mouth together.

Warily, he searched for his wallet to see if he had been robbed but neither his watch nor almost two thousand dollars in cash he carried had been touched.

Confused, Julian sat on the sofa and tried to piece together what had happened but the more he prodded his memory, the more fleeting it became.

It was not until Eloise began to call his phone an hour later that Julian was forced to accept that he had probably made up the black-haired girl in some ecstasy-induced illusion. Even so, Julian couldn't help but feel a bizarre sense of loss as if he had let someone get away even though he had no real way of knowing if she existed.

I

JULIAN

Open.

Closed.

Open.

I waited.

Closed.

Yep, Terry was on a tear that morning although what he had set his sights on, I couldn't say. No one knew what went through that man's mind half the time.

I sighed deeply and turned my attention back to the computer screen, trying to block out my lawyer's obsessive opening and closing of drawers in the next room. It was the downfall of working at the home office—the soundproofing was awful.

Of course, I hadn't expected to have company on the days when I worked from home.

Certainly not my OCD attorney, I thought wryly. It was probably time to remodel the house and add extra insulation. My, how things had changed since my father ran Bryant Land Holdings. His vision of the company had been three high-rise condos on the east coast before the housing market had exploded. It was sad he hadn't lived long enough to see what I had done with his baby.

Now, I was running a multi-billion-dollar empire from the sprawling estate off the coast of Biscayne Bay on my private island. It was supposed to have been a sanctuary, an escape from the skyscrapers and bustle of city life but Terry was making it very difficult to forget the woes which waited for me in the city with all his thumping around in the neighboring office.

Such motion was indicative that something was truly bothering him. I was biding my time because I knew in a matter of minutes, he would be knocking on my door, demanding some piece of paper or another and I would be forced to talk him down. I would need the couple extra minutes to hone my inner Zen for that.

To make matters worse, Eloise was calling—again. I had set my cell ringer to silent but that didn't stop my insane step-sister from continuously phoning as if her persistence was going to break me down and not make me force her to wait longer. How little she knew me.

She hadn't broken me in the twenty years we'd been related and I wasn't losing my edge, no matter how much she wished for it.

No sooner did Eloise give up calling did Terry knock on the door, trading the present mishap with the original.

"Julian? Can I come in?"

It wasn't like he gave me much of a choice and the door flew open, displaying the disheveled lawyer at the threshold.

It truly never ceased to amaze me that a man who made eight figures could perpetually carry the resemblance of a homeless person in Hialeah. In fact, I think I'd seen better put together hobos than Terry. We lived in Florida. The world was our oyster. Even if he wanted to wear khakis and Hawaiian shirts, he could have done it with a modicum of style.

But that was Terry.

"If I say no, will you leave?" I asked hopefully and as always, he ignored me, making his way toward the massive desk which I sat behind. It had belonged to my father and while I personally saw it as an eyesore, it also made me feel closer to the old man. We hadn't been all that tight in my youth. His priorities were as follows: Bryant Land Holdings, Madeline, Bryant Land Holdings, us kids. But I still missed the bastard. He had done his best for me and his wretched wife and step-daughter while he was alive.

No matter what Madeline and Eloise say about him, I thought grimly. They had no problem trashing my father's good name in his death but trashy was what suited the Sinclair women best.

"I can't find the Hoover Street file," Terry explained nervously, pacing around the front of the desk. I half-expected to see him wring his hands like a father waiting in a maternity ward.

"I've looked everywhere, Julian. It's not where it's supposed to be."

I gritted my even, white teeth together and

stifled a groan of annoyance. Like the antique desk, Terry was another throwback from my father's reign at Bryant. I adored the man, sincerely but his old-school mentality drove me to the brink sometimes.

"Terry," I said patiently. "I told you, all the property files have been uploaded into the system for convenience sake. The paper files have been moved into storage in New York. What are you looking for? It's literally at your fingertips, whatever you need."

Terry stared at me blankly and for a moment, I wondered if I have slipped into another language while talking. I was fluent in three but I didn't think that was the problem in that instance.

"What? What, Terry?" I demanded, unable to hide my exasperation. The phone was lighting up again. I wasn't going to get any work done that day, not when I was required to babysit all the pains in my ass at once. I needed an assistant just to wrangle these nitwits.

"I don't understand why we can't just keep the files on hand. It's a huge inconvenience to fly to New York every time I need to look something up."

I stared at him.

"Seriously?" I heard myself ask. I couldn't believe he didn't grasp the concept of what I had just said. A bemused guffaw escaped my lips but it only served to upset Terry more. I quickly stifled my amusement and turned to the computer.

"You don't need to fly to New York, Terry. Everything is at your fingertips. Come here."

I gestured for him to come closer and he shuffled toward me. Through my peripheral vision, I wondered if he thought I was plotting his death. He certainly wore an expression of concern.

"Terry, you're one of the biggest real estate lawyers in the country. How is it that working with technology is such a chore for you?"

He shrugged, a sheepish expression crossing his face.

"Val does everything for me," he replied and I grunted. I wanted to slap some sense into him, to remind him that Bryant Land Holding accounts held proprietary information, things that should not be entrusted to his latest bimbo assistant but I held my tongue. As I said, Terry had been a permanent fixture around the family since before I was born. He hadn't screwed us so far so I had my fingers crossed that beneath his ineptitude for computers, he was still in control of his razor-sharp intuition.

"Are you going to answer that?" Terry asked suddenly, noticing the phone lighting up on my desk.

"It's Eloise," I replied nonchalantly. "Go ahead."

Terry couldn't hide the grimace on his face and I snickered.

"I didn't think so. Here, look." I pointed at the screen, logging in through my admin account and pulling up the Hoover Street property in Washington. It was remarkable that I could keep the land owned by Bryant in my mind. There were hundreds, some with similar sounding names even but I suppose I had learned them by rote as a child. Later, I had acquired more of them on my own. They weren't just buildings and lots to me—people lived there and businesses existed in those structures. I had visited all of them personally and was able to conjure them in my mind's eye when discussing them.

"Here. Everything you need on the property, all right?" I told Terry, sitting back so he could scroll through the information I had found. He blinked with myopic blue eyes and I watched as the widened with wonder.

Oh come on! I grumbled silently. *You can't seriously be this shocked to see this.*

I knew I had personally set him on the computer in this very fashion at least six times previously. Maybe he really was getting too old to retain new knowledge.

They say you can't teach an old dog new tricks. I wonder how accurate that is.

"Fascinating," he murmured and I snorted.

"Not really. It's a spreadsheet."

I left him to look for whatever it was he needed and rose from my high-back leather chair to stretch. I needed an espresso anyway. I could afford to give up my screens for a few minutes.

"I'm grabbing a coffee. Want anything?"

He shook his head, claiming my seat and leaned forward to scroll through the page as I turned to leave the office.

"Your sister's calling again."

The word "sister" caused me to shudder but I didn't bother to correct Terry. It was hard to say if he called Eloise my sister because he believed she was or it was a passive/aggressive stab at annoying me.

Oh, and it did annoy me. Being related to Eloise by blood was almost the worst thing I could imagine. To that day, I couldn't reconcile what my hardworking father had seen in her gold-digging mother.

The apple certainly doesn't fall far from the tree, does it?

Sighing, I whirled back to snatch the phone off the desk. I was going to have to answer sooner or later. Eloise would just jam up my voicemail and block my incoming calls with her persistence. I relented. Better I answer now when I was idle than in the middle of something. Sooner or later I'd be forced to talk to her.

"What?" I snapped, spinning back toward the door.

"And good morning to you too," she purred. "I've been calling you for two days. When did you get home?"

I grunted. I knew she'd been calling for two days. I'd been avoiding her just as long. Moreover, why was she calling me to shoot the breeze? That girl really needed a job. The thing was, the only job she wanted was mine.

"Yesterday. What do you want, Eloise?"

"How was Vegas?" she continued, apparently unwilling to get to the point. I considered disconnecting the call but I reasoned she would just keep at it until I answered again.

"Vegas was Vegas, Eloise," I sighed but as I said it, I was reminded of the dream girl who had flittered in and out of my hotel suite on my last night.

I still couldn't be clear if she was real or not but the horde of new clothes in size four which littered the sitting room told me I had either entertained someone that night or I had been on one hell of a trip.

I hoped it was the former, even if I couldn't remember much about her. Once in a while, I would get a whiff of her cheap but sexy perfume, undoubtedly something from Walmart or the likes. It suited her, not because she had been so obviously without money but because she was so achingly uncomplicated somehow.

So uncomplicated, she didn't even have a name, I thought, mildly irritated with myself for not having learned it. Or maybe I had and forgotten it.

Calling her "Kitten" in my sober, sane mind was horribly embarrassing.

"Hello? Are you still there?" Eloise chirped in my ear and I was forced back to reality.

"Yes, Eloise, I am. What do you want? Why are you calling my phone like a madwoman?"

"Oh, so you did notice me calling," she laughed but as always, there was little mirth in her tone.

"Eloise, can you kindly get to the point?" I sighed, rolling my eyes. "This is getting tedious as always."

"I have a friend I think you should meet," she announced and I snorted with contempt.

"Yeah, that's not going to happen," I told her firmly. "Anything else?"

"I think you should hear me out without reacting," she said in that condescending tone which made me want to reach through the phone and throttle her. "I'm not full of shitty ideas all the time, Julian. How about when I set up the buyout for the Lausanne property. That was a good idea, wasn't it? How come you always dismiss me?"

I rolled my eyes heavenward and prayed for mercy. There was nothing like arguing with a narcissist.

"Fine," I conceded, padding down the floating staircase toward the kitchen. Laura was dusting the front foyer and I grinned lazily at her. She continued to work and I idly wondered why I was surrounded by such unpleasant people. They had always been there, I suppose and had flittered into my subconscious without me noticing. It was a wonder I wasn't more of a bastard.

Not to say I wasn't one.

"People are starting to talk about you, big brother."

"Don't call me that!" I hissed before I could stop myself. I knew she had only said it for a reaction but it did push my buttons.

"Fine," she grunted. "People are starting to talk about you, *Julian.*"

"That's nice," I replied, stifling a yawn of boredom. "I'm glad I make for good subject matter."

I reached for the espresso compressor and ground some beans down. I hoped the noise bothered her.

"It won't be good subject matter when our company takes a hit, Julian."

"Our company?" I echoed in disbelief. She just didn't give up, did she? Never had there been a breath of discussion that Eloise would be involved with Bryant. She was a Sinclair, not a Bryant. I wonder what it was going to take to drive that home.

Probably a two by four.

"Julian, I've been hearing very disturbing rumors about you," she continued, sighing.
"Okay, Eloise, I'll bite. What rumors?"

"People think you're gay, Julian."

I began to laugh, the noise starting in the pit of my belly and flowing upward to escape in amused bursts through my mouth. I had never heard such a ridiculous assessment in my entire life. There was no one in the world who could possibly believe that I, Julian Andrew Bryant, was a homosexual male.

Not that I cared how people chose to live their lives and it wasn't an insult to my masculinity. How could it be? I knew who I was and I loved the female form more than any man I knew. While it tickled me that someone might spark that rumor, I knew there was no validity to it. I had no doubt that my step-sister was talking out of her ass but the amused glee forced me to press her for more details.

"Where did you read this? Is my gay love nest in the National Enquirer?" I snickered. "Oh, wait, who is my lover? Ryan Gosling? Please tell me it's Ryan Gosling?"

I was probably getting too much enjoyment out of the idea but it was truly the first I'd ever heard anything like that and it had been a long while since I'd giggled like a kid.

"People are talking, Julian. You can mock me all you want but you haven't had a girlfriend in years. They're calling you a confirmed bachelor now which is code for—"

"Eloise," I snapped, my good mood evaporating

as I realized she meant whatever she was saying. "Even if this is something that's happening, who gives a shit? It's not true and even if it was, this is 2018. Being gay is hardly the scandal of the century."

"Are you gay? You can tell me. I love you and I will always be here for you—"

"Oh my God! I'm hanging up now."

"No! Wait! Listen to me," she urged. "It's not a big deal what people think in the big cities...I guess although I think you're being a little too liberal minded in my opinion. Even so, think about how many properties we hold in the Bible Belt. Those folks aren't apt to be as forgiving about something like this. It's all about appearances, Julian. Think about the company. People have boycotted business for less than a gay CEO."

I wished she would stop insinuating that Bryant Land Holdings belonged to her also but that was a matter for another time. It dawned on me that her talking like that bothered me more than the apparent rumors about my sexuality.

"Eloise, I am not gay," I said flatly, no longer a

fan of the conversation. "And I think you're blowing this out of proportion."

"I'm sure you're right," she replied but there was no conviction in her voice. "But even if I am, what harm will it do to meet with Genevieve?"

I already hated her friend because I saw how the conversation had gone full circle now.

I'd been taken by Eloise's double talking and landed back where she wanted me.

Genevieve.

"Jule?"

"I'll meet your insipid friend," I growled, eager to get off the phone with her. Suddenly, Eloise's words had filled me with doubts. She was right —like any business, the image of the CEO was everything. I was going to have to talk with the head of PR and Marketing to get a handle on how serious an issue I might have before me.

Gay. Seriously? Of all the dumb ass rumors to have spread about me, that was the last one I was expecting.

But, that was big business after all. I had

learned a long time ago to expect the unexpected.

"Gen is lovely," Eloise chirped. "You two will hit it off, you'll see. And in the end, everyone wins."

I found myself staring at the phone, wondering what my step-sister had to gain from any of this. What did she care if there was gossip about me? No matter how she spun it, the company genuinely had no bearing on her life. There was something else going on there, something playing in the back of her mind.

I knew Eloise Sinclair didn't do anything without a benefit to herself.

2

KENNEDY

"Have you ever tried this?" the lady with the pinched, quavering voice asked and I shook my head. I had a hard time believing she could see the items at all. It was the fourth time she had asked me about a product as if my lowly opinion on whatever garbage can she selected was the end all and be all to her choice that day. She'd already monopolized me for twenty minutes and I eyed my cart longingly. I'd never wanted to put away stock so badly in my life but I could see she needed to be walked through her purchase with kid gloves. Her name was Sue and she came into the store about once a week. Most of the other employees avoided her but I took pity on her sad, elderly heart.

"I've heard good things about that one," I

offered even though I was lying through my teeth. I mean really, who gave feedback on kitchen garbage cans?

"Oh yeah?" Her voice was grating on my nerves and I was reminded of something but before I could grab the elusive thought, it was gone.

"Okay!" she decided cheerfully, reaching for it with frail arms. Instantly, I stepped forward to grab it for her. She had to be pushing eighty and the last thing I wanted was an elderly woman breaking a hip on aisle four.

"I'll get that for you," I told her quickly. "Do you have other items to buy?"

"Oh…"

She stared at me with rheumy red eyes and I could read the confusion in them. Again, my heart cracked for her. She was puzzled, maybe even disoriented.

"Maybe…?"

"I'll bring this up to the cashier and when you're done shopping, you can just go there, all right, ma'am?"

A weak but grateful smile appeared on her face and she nodded.

"Thank you, sweetie. You're so kind and helpful. What's your name?"

She was staring right at my nametag but I doubted very much that she could read the small print with her ancient eyes.

"Kennedy, ma'am."

"Oh. That's a good, strong name," she said, nodding affirmatively. "You're going to be very successful."

I wanted to snicker dubiously but I knew she was being nice. It was hard to envision going places with two minimum wage jobs.

"Have a good day, ma'am."

I turned back to my cart filled with stock and Belle poked her head around the corner, rolling her brown eyes dramatically.

"You got suckered in by Sue, huh?"

"It was fine," I replied and I meant it. The old lady was nothing compared to some of the jackasses I'd tended to in the big box store where I'd worked for almost five years. At least Sue wasn't drunk, trying to steal or grabbing my ass. I'd take Sue any day of the week.

"You've got the patience of a saint," Belle insisted. "I literally run in the other direction when I see her coming. I bet you wish you were back in Vegas right now, dontcha?"

That was the absolute last place I ever wanted to go again but I didn't tell my co-worker that. In her mind, winning that contest on CKOY was a dream come true. I'd won a trip for two and she'd hinted wildly that she wanted to be my plus one but I hadn't taken anyone. The idea had been for me to escape the life I knew in Indiana, if only for four days.

And what a four days it was.

I blushed as I remembered. Or at least tried to remember. I had started drinking on the plane the morning I left. There had been snatches of casinos and hotels, loud music and a man...I think there had been a man.

In my mind's eye, he was tall enough that I had to cock my head back to look up at his face. The vivid aqua eyes had a hypnotic but dream-like quality to them as if he was somewhere else and his hair had almost been as dark as mine but cut stylishly short and swept back against a chiseled face.

Had he taken me shopping? Out for lobster?

Probably not. I'd probably dreamt the entire thing because when I came to on the third day, I was at Circus Circus, alone and without a modicum of self-respect. It was hard to feel prideful with your face pressed to the carpet of your hotel room, your legs twisted beneath you as if you'd fallen and decided to stay there. I'd been on a bender and I didn't remember a damned thing.

I spent the fourth day in Vegas nursing my insane hangover in my room, trying to piece together where I'd been and what I'd done.

Even though I'd been home for a week, I couldn't shake the feeling that some picture of me would pop up on the internet, dancing down the strip in a coconut bra or something equally ridiculous. But so far, whatever trouble I'd found myself in over those three days had not come to surface and I wasn't sure if I was happy or worried about that.

Everyone needs to let loose sometimes, I reminded myself. *You're twenty-five years old and deserve a break from the mundane. Who cares what you did? You're never going to get or seize an opportunity like that again.*

"You haven't said much about your trip," Belle complained and I could see her desire to live vicariously through me. I wished I had the imagination to give her a good story but all I could do was shrug.

"Did you see any shows? Did you go to Caesar's Palace?"

I shook my head in the negative to her questions.

"There's not much to tell," I replied truthfully. "It went by very quickly."

At least those were the facts.

"I think we— "she stopped talking abruptly and turned her head away from me. Instantly I knew our manager had wandered down the aisle. Belle was a sorceress at disappearing when Christine appeared. One day, I vowed to make her tell me her secrets because it seemed like my manager only appeared when I was exactly in the middle of doing something.

"Haven't you had enough time off?" Christine demanded, scowling at me. "I would think you would be grateful your job was still here for you when you came back from your Vegas vacation."

The jealousy in her tone was almost tangible.

Everyone wants to get out of Cedarside, I thought. *But we're all stuck here in our own way.*

Christine had been my manager since I started and in that time had given birth to three children, adding to the two she'd had before I'd known her. Her common-law husband was a long-distance trucker who was apparently only home long enough to get her pregnant before heading out again.

It didn't take a psychologist to figure out that Christine was miserable and I tried to take that into account when she glared at me with those porcine eyes, ready to write me up for no reason. Or at least threaten to write me up. I don't think she ever really had in my entire employment.

She was a bit of a bully, demanding respect because she deemed herself an authority figure but no one much saw her as anything but a pain and hard ass.

"I am very grateful my job is still here," I assured her. "I was just helping a customer and I'm going to finish stocking before clocking out."

"You're not getting paid extra if it takes you longer," Christine spat as if I had begged her for overtime.

"I know," I said quietly. Sometimes I wondered if she was trying to instigate a war with me just to keep her life interesting.

Or maybe just so she would have an excuse to fire me. Perhaps she knew how badly I needed that job and liked to make me work for it but exerting what little power she had. Whatever the reason, I didn't want to rock the boat. And Christine wasn't *that* bad...

Christine grunted and spun to leave me to my work. I had forty-five minutes until my shift was over and I knew I could get the work done—provided Sue didn't come around looking for more help.

"She's such a miserable cow," Belle muttered, sticking her head around the aisle. She hadn't gone far apparently.

"We're all miserable in our own way," I said lightly and Belle snickered.

"You're a poet, Ken. Want to come to karaoke tonight?"

I shook my dark hair.

"I'm working," I told her. "Maybe next time."

"You say that every time!"

"I'm always working!"

There were truths in that. Yes, I did work seven days a week. Some days I worked both jobs or split shifts but if I wanted to maintain my car payment and rent, I didn't have much of a choice.

But I also despised karaoke. I couldn't imagine anything worse than getting on stage in front of a bunch of strangers who were judging your singing. And people paid money to do this!

"Maybe I'll come by the bar after and keep you company."

I glanced up at Belle and smiled.

"That would be good."

Belle waved and skipped away from me, presumably to get back to work but who could really say. She might have been doing her social rounds for all I knew. The girl worked less than anyone I knew.

I moved my eyes back to the shelves and

continued my work. I'd only have two hours between shifts and I was looking forward to running home and having a shower before heading out to work again although I did bring my uniform with me to the store in case I had to stay late. That night really didn't want to be at the store any longer than I had to be, especially if I wasn't getting paid the extra time.

Out of the corner of my eye, I saw Sue shuffling by with her cart, looking lost and I paused, debating whether to engage her. It would undoubtedly take another twenty minutes to orient the old woman but I couldn't in good conscience watch her amble around without direction.

"Ma'am, do you need any more help?" I called to her. I hoped Belle wasn't in earshot. I'd never hear the end of it for volunteering my time.

Sue looked around as if she thought God was speaking to her from above and I suppressed a sigh and walked toward her. Gently, I placed a hand on her arm and she jerked as if I'd burned her.

"I'm sorry. I didn't mean to startle you."

"Oh. No, no, dear. I'm looking for the kitchen

garbage cans. I need a kitchen garbage can. Do you know where I can find one?"

I pursed my lips together and offered her a smile.

"You already selected one, ma'am. I put it at the register for you already. Would you like me to show you where it is?"

Consternation filled her face and I was immediately struck with sympathy for her. Once upon a time, she probably held a job, raised a family, maybe even owned a house. Now she was wandering through a store, relying on strangers for help.

And some of those strangers are ignoring her even. God, is this the life I have to look forward to?

I seemed to be headed in that direction.

"Are you sure?" Sue asked suspiciously. "I don't remember you getting me a garbage can. Are you sure?"

"Yes ma'am. Let me show you."

Reluctantly, she allowed me to lead her toward the front of the store and I pointed at the register where I'd left her can. Her eyes narrowed.

"I don't like that one," she told me decisively. "I want another one."

I heard a chuckle behind me but I didn't need to turn around to know it was Belle.

"Of course," I told her. "Let's find you one you prefer."

We made our way back to the aisle and I glanced covertly at my watch. Something told me that I was not going to have a chance to go home between shifts. I'd have to go right from the store to the bar that night.

Nothing new there, I thought grimly. *Just another day in the life of the bottom 99%.*

∽

IT WAS ALMOST THREE A.M. WHEN I STUMBLED into my three storey walk-up downtown. My legs felt like rubber and when I finally unlocked both deadbolts and fell inside the apartment, I collapsed onto the worn futon I used as a couch in a heap.

The night had been unusually busy and Belle had stopped by as promised but she had caused me more grief than companionship, thanks to the pre-drinks she'd had at karaoke.

In between me running out drink orders and tending bar, I was forced to listen to Belle gripe about everything from her parents to our work. She even managed to throw some shade on her current boyfriend and by last call, I was sure that my exhaustion was more emotional than it was physical.

I didn't have a lot in common with Belle after all. She still lived at home, worked at the store for extra cash but her parents paid for everything. She had a boyfriend. She had everything I could probably have ever wanted in the world and yet she still complained. It made my head hurt.

Note to self: next time Belle offers to come by, make up an excuse to keep her away.

I closed my eyes without effort, the lids magnetized to one another in my fatigue. Blissfully, I didn't work until noon the following day so at least I'd be permitted some sleep to recoup some of my energy.

But instead of the warm cloak of slumber

encasing me, the man from Vegas popped into my mind with blinding clarity.

From behind my closed lids, I could make out every feature of his devastatingly handsome face, the glimmer of his sea-colored eyes, the upturn of his nose. There was something hauntingly familiar about that fine jaw and broad forehead but nothing I could glean in my exhausted state.

He's probably a movie star or musician, I realized and humiliation crept through me at the realization that I was having some childish fantasy that I had mixed into reality. But even with the embarrassment, I couldn't deny the surge of heat which pulsated through me and I shifted slightly, my eyes still closed but so I lay on my back. I hadn't even bothered to kick off my shoes but that seemed decidedly less important than addressing the warmth between my legs.

Flashes danced through my mind. The taste of champagne on moist lips intertwined with the scent of musky aftershave flooded me and my fingers rubbed on the outside of my panties. A tooth found my lower lip, my forearm tensing as more memories sifted through the holes of that trip.

Me on my knees inside a gorgeous hotel suite, surrounded by marble and modern furniture. His hands entwined in my hair, rocking me slowly against him as I took him fully into the back of my throat. He was bigger than any man I'd ever been with and I was thinking about how he'd feel inside me.

The thought drenched me both in the reality of my apartment and the fantasy of that hotel suite I must have concocted in my mind.

I moaned softly, feeling the slickness of my center. Two digits moved evenly against my opening and I begged myself to recall more about him but I was too caught up in my current pleasure to search for details too deeply.

Harder my fingertips worked, slipping and sliding over my throbbing nub and when I plunged myself inside myself, I was ready to release.

With a shuddering sigh, I spilled over my own hand but even as I lay quivering in the aftermath of my orgasm, I did not open my eyes. How could I? I could still see his gorgeous face staring back at me. Reality or not, it was the one good thing I'd experienced all day and I wasn't letting it go for anything.

3

JULIAN

To say I was bored was perhaps the biggest understatement to ever leave my lips. For over a week, Eloise's words about the rumors circulating about me had been weighing on my mind and I began to investigate the truth behind them.

As it turned out, my evil step-sister had been telling the truth about them. Nothing had gotten out of hand so far but there was enough floating around on the world wide web to cause me some concern and I called a meeting with Jessica Lynch and Harvey Mathis from PR and Marketing.

"Oh yeah," Jessica commented lightly on the phone. "I heard about that too."

"You heard about that and didn't think you should mention it to me?" I asked, shaking my head in disbelief.

"Julian, darling, do you have any idea how many unfounded rumors float around about you and your family day-to-day? If I came to you with every single thing that crossed my ears, you'd never be able to conduct business."

I wonder what she's heard about Eloise. I'll have to pick her brain one day and find out.

"Jessica, this is something that could cost us tenants," I told her grimly. "And it needs to be nipped in the bud."

"All right," she replied agreeably and I wondered if she hadn't already decided to come to me before I beat her to the punch. "What would you like to do?"

"That's your damned job!" I growled, pounding a fist against the desk in frustration. Sometimes I felt like I was the only one who earned their check at the end of the day.

"Let's have a sit-down," she said in her maternal, soothing tone. "It's not that bad."

"Not yet," I retorted. "Let's make sure it doesn't get any worse."

But as I sat staring at the new marketing strategy Harvey had laid out, focusing on families and therefore subliminally indicating that I was of traditional values, I wanted to go to sleep.

Still, I knew that both of the people sitting before me were highly capable and knew how to perform damage control.

"It wouldn't hurt if you found yourself a steady girlfriend," Jessica offered, perhaps sensing me zoning out of the meeting. The words shocked me back into the present.

"Do people even say 'steady' anymore?" I jibed back although I felt a hot flush of embarrassment creep up my neck.

What is wrong with you? I demanded of myself. *Since when does the mention of a girlfriend make you blush?*

Over the years there had been models and actresses, bankers, lawyers and debutantes. I had never had a shortage of female admirers or accessible dates but suddenly, the task seemed a huge burden for some reason I couldn't fathom.

Fleetingly, a shot of silken black hair crossed my vision before it was gone again.

Am I holding out for a mystery girl?

The idea seemed laughable. There was still no concrete proof that she had existed and even though I had been very tempted to call the hotel and ask for footage of that night, if only to put my mind to rest, I did not.

If she did exist, whatever fun we had stayed in Vegas just like everyone else. Anyway, you were so high on E, you have no idea if you picked up a troll from under a bridge. It's probably best to leave well enough alone.

Still, I couldn't deny that my curiosity was piqued over the matter.

"Why are you deflecting?" Jessica asked pointedly, drawing me back to the matter at hand. "You've never struck me as the type to have a problem finding a girlfriend, Julian. Unless…"

She trailed off and for the first time in my life, I saw her look uncomfortable.

"*Are* you gay?"

I grunted in exasperation. If one more person asked me that question, I was going to lose my mind. I still couldn't reconcile how such a rumor had started.

"I assure you, if I was, I would not hide it from my shareholders or tenants. But I am not. In fact, I have a date this weekend. With a woman, in case you were wondering."

I didn't but I could quickly see things were about to implode among my own people. One of the worst things about being the boss was having to give the peasants what they wanted or public opinion was going to turn and once that happened, there would be a very slim hope of recovery. I had to keep everyone united and confident that the rumors were unfounded—starting with my team.

Jessica's face relaxed in relief.

"You know if you were, Julian, we would—"

"I'm not!"

I heard the defensiveness in my voice and I wondered what it would sound like to her.

This is absurd. All over a stupid rumor. I'm annoyed that this is annoying me. It's like someone telling you you're an apple and you're trying to explain to them you're human but their minds are made up.

"All right. Let's hope the girl this weekend is 'the one', "Jessica chuckled and turned back to Harvey. "Let's focus on the campaign, all right?"

They continued to drone on around me and I sat back in my chair, my shoulders sinking. I hadn't even realized I'd had my back up. The boredom ensued from there, the campaign making me bleary eyed. I tried to move my thoughts elsewhere.

I had to find a date for the weekend.

Instantly, I considered going back to Vegas and I was again filled with shame. What the hell was wrong with me? I couldn't get this ghost of a woman out of my mind. For all I knew, I was stuck on a hallucination.

My cell rang and of course it was Eloise.

"I'm in a meeting," I told her. "I'll call you later."

"No you won't," she replied sweetly and I was almost impressed with how well she knew me. "Why don't we just talk while I have you on the line."

"What do you want, Ellie?" I knew my nickname for her gave her anxiety but for once, she didn't take the bait.

"Mom told me to ask you over for dinner tonight."

I ground my teeth together. The only thing I could think of that was worse than seeing Eloise was seeing Eloise and Madeline in one spot.

"I'm sorry, I—"

"We already called your secretary and we know you have nothing scheduled tonight," my stepsister told me crisply. "Seven o'clock. Bring a Chianti."

She disconnected the call before I could respond and I stared at the phone hatefully. It had been months since I'd been forced through a dinner at the Sinclair's house.

It really is the Sinclair house now, isn't it?

I hadn't given it much thought but Madeline had insisted on keeping her ex-husband's last name when she married my father. Now with him gone, the house no longer belonged to the Bryants. I got the company and Moochy Maddy got everything else. I wondered if she had wiped all trace of my father from the mansion in Miami Beach. It was reason enough to attend that night, I figured. See if there were any old pictures of my dad still kicking around or had the two witches had a massive bonfire and sacrificed a goat?

Madeline was just like her daughter—insistent, petulant and would stop at nothing to get what she wanted. If I refused dinner that night, she would just hound me until I came. But if I went, it would buy me a few more months of peace thereafter. Anyway, there was probably an ulterior motive to the invite and finding out what those were was always fun.

"Girlfriend?" Jessica teased and I smiled tightly, dropping the phone on the table before me.

"Eloise."

"Ah."

Jessica immediately turned back to Harvey and it gave me a feeling of comfort to know I wasn't the only one who despised my step-sister.

Eloise just had that effect on people.

∽

I DON'T KNOW WHY I TOOK THE PORCHE TO

the mansion. It was the fastest car I owned and the ride seemed to take three minutes. I should have walked.

Yet at five to seven, I was setting off the intercom sensor and waiting for the butler to respond to my arrival. I hadn't bothered with the wine. If they had cleaned out my dad's prized wine cellar already, they didn't deserve another bottle.

I have to announce myself at my father's house. What a fucking joke.

"Please come in, Mr. Bryant," Jeffery intoned without preamble. He recognized me through the camera. The butler had been with my family since my mom was alive and I had always liked him. I had invited the old man to come and work on my island after my dad died but he refused. I had no idea if he did it out of some old world British loyalty thing or because he genuinely liked working for Madeline although I found that impossible to believe. She was insufferable.

I pulled the burgundy car up the half-mile entrance, the sun splaying its rays over the delicately landscaped lawns on either side and to the south of the property, I could see the sparkle of the water beyond the plantation style-house.

There were three cars already in the drive and I felt my back tense slightly. They hadn't mentioned company.

Not that I expected anything but the unexpected from the Sinclairs.

They are full of surprises...among other things.

Jeffery appeared at the door even before I exited my car and he hurried toward me. For a shocking second, I thought he looked terrified, his green eyes encircled in dark shadows and lines etched into his weathered face which hadn't been there before. As I was going to ask if he was all right, his eyes brightened and there was suddenly no trace of the scared man I'd seen before.

"Welcome, Mr. Bryant."

"You know, Jeffery, you used to change my diapers," I commented dryly. "I'm still good if you call me Julian."

It was a conversation we'd had at least one hundred thousand times in the past but the man was far too cultured to do any such thing.

The elderly man opened his mouth to respond but his words were swallowed by another.

"Jeffery knows his place, Julian," a cold voice said before emerging from the dark shadows of foyer. "He would never cross the line, would you, Jeffery."

"If only we could all claim the same, Maddy," I replied tightly. "How are you?"

I stared at her with mild disgust, wondering if she ever truly looked at herself in the mirror before showing her face to the world. She was the poster child for cosmetic surgery gone wrong. A set of duck lips emanated from a chin much too small to sustain her and her fair cheeks were rouged bright pink, presumably to hide the scars of the numerous lifts she'd undergone over the years.

She flowed toward me in a dressing gown that some starlet from the fifties would wear but I casually stepped out of her impending embrace. The idea of touching her repelled me in ways I couldn't explain. Ever since I was a child, being near Maddy and her overpowering perfume made me gag.

It's funny what you pick up as a child, like your

sixth sense has been unblemished by bias and manipulation. You just know when someone isn't right.

Maddy was that someone to me.

My dad thought it was because I was worried she was trying to replace my mom but there was no competition there. They were two very different people.

It wasn't just that Maddy was physically unappealing. It was the blackness of her heart which struck me the most.

"Oh," Madeline sighed in answer to my question. "I've been much better but you would know that if you came around more often. You don't even answer your emails, Julian. It's like you don't care."

I had prepared myself for her pseudo guilt-trip. After twenty years, it was the same thing every time he was forced to see her.

"Well you know, Maddy, the company isn't going to run itself. Or do you know that?"

I stared at her inquisitively. Maybe she really thought the company ran itself like a machine. Who knew if anything at all was happening behind those sooty eyes, so akin to her daughter's.

Her eyes narrowed and her mouth puckered into a pout which was truly a hideous expression given the duck lips. I had to look away.

"Of course you're busy," she spat back. "We all are."

I bit back the pressing question of what it was exactly that she did. As far as I knew, she invested in plastic surgery and personal trainers. Hell, even her wretched daughter ran charity events on behalf of Bryant Land Holdings but I suspected that Eloise did that solely so she could keep a pinky toe in the door of the company.

"Your sister and friends wait for you in the parlor."

The parlor. She really does want people to believe that she's from another century.

"Sounds swell," I couldn't resist saying. I followed her inside, Jeffery on my heels and I turned back to cast him another look. I couldn't shake the feeling that he was trying to communicate something to me but what it was, I couldn't decipher.

Inside the main floor living room, Eloise stood by the bar, caught up in some long-winded story and two others stood nearby, hanging on her every word. When her eyes fell on him, she abruptly stopped talking and grinned warmly, her sooty eyes glowing in a way which made me uncomfortable.

"Ah, here's the man of the hour," she cooed. "Come in, Julian."

"Gee, thanks," I offered sarcastically, trying to swallow my annoyance at being invited into my own father's house. "I'll see if I can find my way around."

Eloise skillfully sidestepped my caustic comment and turned to her friends.

"Genevieve Brulle, this is my brother, Julian Bryant. Julian, Genevieve."

I should have known.

Of course.

I had been so consumed with everything going on, I had forgotten about Genevieve. I don't know why I didn't clue in sooner. There was ulterior motive number one.

It was going to be a short dinner.

The redhead turned and beamed at me with luminous green eyes, extending a pale hand.

"Your photos online don't do you justice," she demurred. I stared at her fingers and glanced at their companion who stood off to the side quietly.

"You really can take the girl out of the trailer park," I commented harshly, ignoring Genevieve's palm. "But you can't take the trailer park out of the girl. Your etiquette still suffers, my ghetto relations."

I strode toward the silent girl who gaped at me in surprise.

"Julian Bryant," I introduced. "Eloise's *step-brother*."

I didn't need to turn around to know I was being glowered at by not just Eloise but by my blind date. I didn't care. Being blindsided was not something I appreciated and I intended to show Eloise that I couldn't be handled no matter how hard she tried.

4

KENNEDY

I bolted awake sometime in the middle of the night. I wasn't sure the exact time but I was seized by a nausea so strong, it was reminiscent of my one and only encounter with tequila when I was sixteen.

I barely made it to the bathroom and as I retched, my head began to pound.

Uh, I'm sick, I thought miserably. There is nothing in the world a lower-class person wants to realize less than that they are sick. We can't afford it. We don't have the luxury of using sick days as we're dispensable. For every one of me, there are ten more waiting for my job. Sick is not an option.

I can't be sick. I won't be.

I vomited twice more before I felt the sensation passing but the dizziness remained and my body was hot and achy.

What did I have to take for a flu?

I dug through the medicine cabinet in the dark, moving things around. I was opening the store in the morning. If I popped something and went back to bed, I might be okay when I woke up.

But only if I had something to take.

I found a bottle of Tylenol which had expired and some rubbing alcohol. I highly doubted that was going to kill whatever bug was in my system.

I made my way back to the single mattress which I called a bed and lay on my back, concentrating on my breathing. Sometimes it helped to alleviate nausea but even as I lay there, I realized that I wasn't feeling nearly as bad as I had when I woke.

The time on my alarm read 3:23 a.m. I needed to be up at 5 to open the store for 6. It almost defeated the purpose of going back to bed for an hour but what else was I going to do? An hour and a half wasn't enough time to binge watch anything good on Netflix.

I didn't move. Instead, I lay there with my eyes closed and listened to the sound of my heart thumping in my ears.

Deep breaths, I coached myself. *In and out. Deep breathing.*

I smirked to myself, realizing how much I must sound like a Lamaze instructor. Just as quickly as the smirk appeared, it froze and faded completely.

That's a weird thought to have, I told myself tersely. *Lamaze instructor. I could have thought yoga instructor instead.*

But I knew where it had come from.

I was three weeks late.

You're not pregnant, I scolded myself as a combination of hot and cold washed through me, fighting to humiliate and shock me simultaneously. *You have to have sex to get pregnant and you're a born-again virgin. You haven't had sex since you and Tom and that was over a year ago.*

As if I'd spoken the magic words, it came flooding back to me in a torrent.

I was on my knees, his nakedness flaunting itself boldly in front of my face without shame. I wanted to taste him so badly but I was seeing double. God, I was drunk. Was he as drunk as me? Or was he drunk at all?

I hadn't been paying attention to anything but the curve of his lips, the timbre of his voice and the way his eyes bored into mine. Suddenly, all I could think was how much I wanted that huge, swollen cock inside me, filling every inch of my core.

Even as I thought it, I felt a drip out from my panties and make its way down my thigh. I grabbed him and slid him fully into my mouth. Into my throat I felt him, my cheeks closing around to suction him tightly and I choked on him slightly.

He let out a low groan, gently forcing my head forward until his sack touched my chin.

It was becoming difficult to breathe but I felt him growing harder, bigger and fuller inside my mouth.

"Ah fuck, Kitten!" he moaned. "You're going to make me blow."

The words excited me and suddenly I was bobbing against him, willing him to cum for me but without warning, I was pushed backward and pinned to the ground mercilessly. His cock jabbed at my upper thigh and his own juices were already dripping for me.

Two palms found the backs of my knees and I was spread apart, my eyes fixed on his. Our gazes locked, the thrust of his engorged unit so close, just a thin layer of lace between us.

To my shock, he plunged forward, his fingers gripping my legs so tightly, I was sure there would be bruises. I heard the rip of my underwear as the head of his cock fought its way toward my slick middle. I'd never had anyone do that before!

He was huge and I was throbbing, pulsating against him. I didn't think he would fit but slowly, deeply, he made it happen and I screamed with pleasure when the entire ten inches filled me into my abdomen.

I clenched around him, feeling him rise further and my fingers dug into the muscled blades of his shoulders.

Again I cried out but now he was not being soft but hard and primitive, jabbing into me as if he could wait no longer. It took four slides before my own climax mounted and I spilled onto him in a gush of warmth, tears rolling down my cheeks but my release was met with his.

In hot spurts of lava, his seed filled me, overflowing and joining in mine in a mess of sweat and fluid.

My eyes flew open and I sat up, sweat touching my forehead. I didn't have to double check. I could smell my own wetness through the boxers I had gone to bed in. I was aroused and confused.

Had he really been real?

For weeks I had convinced myself that none of it was real, that I had wasted my expense paid trip to Vegas on binge-drinking and being pathetic and that I had concocted the sexy dark-haired stranger as a way to alleviate that guilt.

But if I was pregnant, there was only one possibility as to who the father could be—the mystery man from Vegas.

I threw my legs over the side of the mattress and scrounged around for my work uniform. I was going in early.

God, I needed to do laundry. How did it all pile up so fast?

There were benefits to working in a box store. Not a lot but once in a blue moon, it came in handy that everything I could be found within the walls of Sav-A-Bunch.

Things like flu medicine.

And pregnancy tests.

I got dressed without turning on the lights. I didn't even bother to check my reflection in the mirror because my looks were the least of my concern at that moment.

Slamming out of the apartment, I bolted down the stairs as fast as my legs would take me. Another bout of dizziness threatened me at the bottom of the stairs and I had to remind myself to take it easy.

Either I was sick or carrying a kid. In both cases, I would need to watch it with overextending myself.

I paused to catch my breath and when I was confident that the vertigo had passed, I continued into the parking lot where my second-hand Ford Fusion sat inconspicuously.

There was no traffic at that hour and aside from the usual suspects loitering around selling something unsavory on the corners, I was virtually alone on the streets.

I made my way to work in ten minutes and with trembling hands, I let myself inside.

The cleaning staff had already deactivated the alarm and one guy still lingered near the employee entrance as if wanting to get every last second on his punch card.

He looked at me shamefully when I appeared and I'm sure my expression told the same story.

We both had something to hide which made us allies.

I gave him a brief, sheepish grin.

"Morning," I offered.

"Hola," he replied and we both parted ways from there.

Some of the lights were on but I didn't need a stage light to guide my way to the pharmacy section of the store. I'd been an employee there for five years. I knew my way to every section in the dark and blindfolded.

I grabbed the first box I saw, not bothering to check its price or accuracy. There were two tests in the box and surely two tests couldn't be wrong.

I'd pay for it later when the registers opened and no one would notice a charge like that at 4 o'clock in the morning.

In seconds I was in the bathroom, huddled in a stall and of course I had stage fright. It took me several minutes of talking nicely to my bladder to instigate any movement and finally, I managed to do what I had to do.

Waiting was the worst part. Two minutes felt like two hours. I kept expecting Christine to burst through the bathroom door and yell, "I know what you're doing in there, Kennedy! Everyone knows!"

In my mind's eye, she pinned a scarlet letter on me or walked me through the store naked, chanting, "Shame!" while customers threw produce at me.

But the guilty mind always thinks things like that...I guess. I've never been one to have a twisted conscience.

What do you even have to feel guilty about? You did nothing wrong...except get drunk and forget who you slept with. It happens on Maury every damn day!

My pep talks weren't helping and I wondered who I could call on to walk me through this but there was no one. No family, no friends. No one but Belle who would likely just tell the entire store and hassle me until I told her the entire sordid story.

I clung to the fact that I still felt feverish. That had to be a sign that I just had the flu, didn't it? Morning sickness didn't come with fever, did it? I had no idea. Outside of biology and health classes, I knew very little about pregnancy.

In my twenty-five years on earth, I'd never had a pregnancy scare. Of course, I'd only ever been with three men—well, four if Vegas guy was not a figment of my imagination.

I'd never considered myself an overly sexual person and it had probably led to the demise of my relationships. If I had the choice between watching a movie or having sex, I would have always picked the movie.

Although the way you acted in Vegas was highly sexual, wouldn't you say?

Was it the booze? The atmosphere? The guy?

Probably a combination of the three. I thought about how the mere idea of that man sent shocks of warmth through me. I'd never felt that way about any of my exes. With them, sex had been a chore, something I did to keep the relationship going. I'd certainly never instigated it the way I had with Vegas guy.

I realized I'd been lost in thought for a while and I dare to look down at the plastic stick in my hand.

Two lines.

I was pregnant.

But I was Kennedy Christensen. I wasn't going to take the word of one piece of plastic made in China. No, I needed two pieces of plastic made in China for confirmation. Shit, I might even need four pieces of plastic made in China. Or maybe I just wasn't ever going to accept it.

I didn't know why I even bothered. I knew in my heart what it was going to say but I was nothing if not thorough.

The second test told the same story as the first.

I sank back against the cold tile wall and tried to evaluate what I'd just learned.

It defied logic that me of all people would find herself in such a position.

I was boring, poor, methodical.

You can't be that methodical, I thought, sitting

straight, my face paling as the severity of the situation came crashing down around my head. *I don't even know my baby daddy's first name. Isn't that kinda the first rule of being organized? Know who the players are?*

That time, I was expecting the vomit when it came.

**End of Sneak Peek: Look for *Accidental Soulmates* on Amazon now

ALSO BY NICOLE CASEY

All my books are either FREE or available in Kindle Unlimited!

Baby Fever (COMPLETED)
Leaving to Stay
Accidental Soulmates
Can't Get Over You
Marrying the Wrong Twin
Deep in the Mountains

The Viera Triplets (COMPLETED)
Dirty Pleasures: A Dad's Best Friend Romance
Come Closer: A Romantic Suspense
Six Years Later: A Second Chance Romance

Beauty & The Captor (COMPLETED)
Her Beast: A Dark Romance

Her Savior: A Dark Romance
Her Dom: A Dark Romance

Standalone
A Weekend with the Mountain Man
Snow and the Seven Men

Romance Collection
Mercury Billionaires
Love, Again

ABOUT THE AUTHOR

Nicole Casey is a Contemporary Romance Author born and based in The City of Angels. She writes steamy contemporary romance with a happily ever after.

When she isn't penning sultry scenes, Nicole Casey loves getting lost in her daydreams, going for long nighttime walks, and fine dining. She is also a red wine aficionada and bookworm. Above all, she enjoys nothing more than spending quality time with her loved ones in both human and cat form.

Subscribe to Nicole Casey's newsletter to get her steamy romance story and be the first to hear about new releases: https://dl.bookfunnel.com/lzcjb30i6u